HEARTS ARE WILD

NO MORE TALKING & DARE YOU TO

RHIAN CAHILL

Hearts Are Wild
By Rhian Cahill
Copyright © 2019 Rhian Cahill
ISBN: 978-1-925375-18-3
Electronic Editions
No More Talking Copyright © 2015 Rhian Cahill
Dare You To Copyright © 2015 Rhian Cahill

All rights reserved. No part of this book may be reproduced, scanned, or distributed in any printed or electronic form without permission. Please do not participate in or encourage piracy of copyrighted materials in violation of the author's rights.

This is a work of fiction. Names, places, characters and incidents are the product of the author's imagination and are fictitious. Any resemblance to actual persons, living or dead, events or establishments is solely coincidental.

For more information visit:
www.rhiancahill.com

NO MORE TALKING

This one's for TimTam for renting a house for the weekend and getting married on the beach.
For Mr.C. Thank you for always believing.

1

ZAC TOOK a deep breath and tried to ignore the woman standing beside him. He'd be fucked if he let her get to him. Again. He faced forward. Stared at the two people standing barefoot in the sand only a few feet away and wondered how soon he could leave. But then he remembered why he was here. Why he stood next to the sweet smelling female who'd starred in every one of his recent fantasies.

Red.

He closed his eyes and breathed through his mouth to stop any more of her tantalizing scent seeping inside and short-circuiting his good intentions. He'd let that happen once before. Memories bombarded him. His eyes shot open, but the sight of West and Kelsey exchanging their vows didn't eradicate the reel of X-rated images playing through his mind.

Six months.

Six months had passed, and every single second was as vivid as though it were only minutes ago he'd given in to the unrelenting attraction that seemed to have sprung up overnight.

Zac didn't know why Frederica Mann had gone from being

his best friend's little sister to the woman he couldn't get out of his head. All he knew was two years ago his libido had taken notice in a way it never had before. And he was fine with that. Completely prepared to ignore the gut-scrapping lust he suddenly felt whenever he looked at Freddie.

Until last March.

He'd answered a call for help from his sister, Cassie, and found himself working alongside Freddie. He'd had it all under control until he'd caught her looking at him as though she wanted to eat him whole. In that instant, he'd been dead in the water and known it.

He hadn't been able to walk away when he should have.

Hadn't been able to keep his hands—his mouth—off her.

One night and she'd ruined him. They hadn't even had sex, but what they had done was the most sexually charged erotic encounter he'd ever experienced. She'd blown more than his cock. She'd blown his mind. But he couldn't—*shouldn't*—be with her. She was West's sister. His *best friend's* little sister.

That's when he'd started thinking of Freddie as Red. Red meant danger—keep clear, stay away—and Zac needed every reminder he could give himself to keep his distance.

Fuck. He may have kept away, but that hadn't stopped him from thinking about her. It was a good thing West couldn't read minds. The dirty thoughts Zac had about Red were bad enough. If his friend ever found out Zac had touched her...that he relived every nanosecond over and over while jerking off...

No matter how badly he wanted Red, he couldn't have her. Except now that he'd had a taste of her, no other woman interested him. Zac would laugh if it weren't for the blue balls he was living with.

She shifted beside him and the sand beneath her feet gave way a little, toppling her in his direction. Her arm brushed his, and in spite of the loud voice screaming in his head not to touch her, he did.

He slipped his arm around her waist to steady her. Warm bare skin met his forearm and Zac's whole body tightened.

Fuck.

He'd forgotten about the backless dress she was wearing to her brother's wedding. The minute he'd seen Red in the sexy blue number, Zac had cursed. She was going to kill him.

Red stiffened against him. She sucked in a breath, her chest rising and thrusting her breasts higher. He couldn't have stopped his gaze from dropping to her generous cleavage if his life depended on it. The lush mounds had felt so right in his hands—under his tongue. His mouth went dry and his cock throbbed as memories of playing with her tits bombarded him.

Zac swallowed, the raw tightness of his throat making it difficult. "You okay?" he asked, his voice a hoarse rasp.

She pulled from his grip. "Fine."

He took a half step away. Her tone and posture spoke volumes about her reaction to their first meeting in six months. She was angry. Rightly so.

Zac had no idea how he'd managed to keep from coming face-to-face with her since March. Luck and survival instinct possibly. And fear. Definitely fear. He'd never had a woman get under his skin the way Red did. She'd been in his life since he'd walked into the first day of preschool and met her brother, but it wasn't until the night of her twenty-fifth birthday that something had changed.

She'd changed from being West's sister to a desirable woman in front of his eyes.

He'd done the right thing—ignored the attraction. For months, he'd managed to pretend he didn't want her. That his mouth didn't water—his groin didn't throb—every time he saw her. Thought about her. And what had those long months gotten him? Nothing but a severe case of blue balls and a craving that burned hotter than ever. He wasn't the type to lie to himself—was usually a straight shooter who valued honesty —except when it came to this lust he had for Red.

Lying over and over again, he'd denied, ignored and crushed the unfamiliar hunger she now inspired.

He knew his reluctance to take what he wanted had to do with who she was along with the small part of him that struggled with the change in his perception of Red. She'd always been West's little sister, and getting his head around the fact that he now wanted to nail her against a wall had him twisted in knots just as much as the belly-clawing lust.

Dragging a hand down his face, he blew out a breath. He wasn't sure he could keep this up. Even now, he wanted to push her to the sand and strip off that flirty little dress so he could get at what lay underneath. Press his lips to the heat between...

Applause and cheers broke out around him, and Zac realised he'd been so lost in his thoughts that he'd missed his best friend's wedding. *Shit.* He needed to forget Red. Ignore the way she looked walking towards her brother and his new wife—her sweet arse swaying side-to-side with each step of those long sexy legs.

Heat and blood filled his groin and his cock grew thick and heavy as his gaze followed Red. He couldn't seem to drag his eyes away. Not until people—his friends—moved between him and her. Someone elbowed him.

"The wedding got you all choked up?" Coop asked with a grin.

Zac shook his head. "What? No."

"Then what the hell are you standing here staring into space for?"

He gave a grunt. His brother had a knowing smirk on his face and Zac had no intention of getting into any kind of conversation with Coop. "I'm going to congratulate the bride and groom."

Before Coop could reply, Zac moved through the crowd towards West and Kelsey. It wasn't until he was shaking his best friend's hand that he noticed Red had disappeared. He couldn't stop himself from scanning the group until his eyes landed on her strawberry-blonde head. Her back was to him as she headed across the patio of the rental house where West and Kelsey's wedding and reception was being held. As he watched her go, Zac came to a life-altering conclusion.

He wasn't going to keep his hands off her.

FREDDIE WATCHED as her brother pulled Kelsey into his arms. You'd have to be blind not to see how in love they were. Zachary Moreland cut across her line of sight, bursting the bubble of happiness her brother's wedding day had given her. She frowned. He was ignoring her like he had for the last six months. Not that it had been hard to ignore her when he miraculously vanished every time she got within shouting distance.

Until today.

Today, he couldn't avoid her, but he sure as hell could pretend she didn't exist.

She still wasn't sure what had gone wrong on that warm autumn night back in March. They'd been all over each other. Then something had happened—changed—and Zac's interest had gone from I-can't-get-enough to I-can't-run-fast-enough. Freddie sighed. She'd never understand the male species.

"What's got you brooding in the corner?" Shaye asked as she handed Freddie a glass of champagne.

"Nothing. Just thinking about how we wouldn't be here if those two hadn't managed to work things out." Freddie tipped her chin in West and Kelsey's direction.

"Mmm...sure, that'll put a frown on your face."

Freddie wasn't about to bite. For a start, Shaye was Kelsey's best friend and not hers. Not to mention part of the tightknit group that Zac hung out with. Plus, she'd always kept things close to her chest. After the drama of her teenage years, Freddie preferred not to air her personal matters in public. Having everyone know her business wasn't something she wanted to deal with ever again.

She took a sip of the cool bubbly liquor and continued to watch the happy couple.

Shaye waited a few more minutes. The two of them stood silently as the party carried on around them until Shaye sighed. "Fine. Let's go over there. Cooper looks like he's having way too much fun, and you know how I like to be his personal party pooper."

With a smile, Freddie let a grinning Shaye drag her across the room to the patio where a group of West and Kelsey's friends were in an animated discussion about the latest blockbuster movie.

She managed to lose herself in the conversation and revelry for about an hour. But the second Zac wandered over and joined the group, Freddie's skin prickled with awareness. It didn't matter how much she wanted to hate Zac for the way he'd treated her since they'd hooked up, her body came alive with need so sharp it stole her breath.

He sat at her feet and brushed his hand against her ankle, causing her to shiver and remember with complete detail just how well he could use his hands. The next few minutes were torturous. She tried to concentrate on the conversation, but all her brain cells were focused on the man at her feet and the memory of what he'd done the last time he'd been there.

Zac shifted and pressed his arm against her leg, his warmth seeping deep beneath her skin. Freddie trembled. He leaned into her and it was all she could do to keep breathing normally. The man was driving her insane without effort. She needed to get away from him before she did something foolish like throw herself into his lap and beg him to finish what they'd started all those months ago and fuck her.

Whistles and clapping erupted and Freddie turned to see her brother carrying Kelsey into the house. With a smile, she faced the group once more, only to be pinned beneath Zac's stare. His gaze drilled into hers and he didn't need to say a word for her to know what he was thinking.

His eyes blazed with heat so intense that every part of her seized—burned. Her throat constricted, her lungs refused to pull air in or push it out, and her pussy clenched in rolling waves that squeezed moisture from her body and drenched her inner thighs. She'd foregone underwear in favour of a panty-line-free outfit and now regretted it. If she didn't get up, there'd be a telltale wet spot on the back of her dress.

"Excuse me." Freddie pushed to her feet and stepped over Zac's outstretched legs. She couldn't miss the way he slid his hand along the back of her calf as she passed and didn't have a hope in hell of stopping her body's reaction to that simple caress.

Walking briskly, Freddie headed for the bedroom she'd be staying in tonight. West and Kelsey were leaving early in the morning for their honeymoon and she'd promised to take care of clean up and returning the keys to the estate agent. It went against every principle she had, but if she had to, she'd hide out in her room until everyone left.

She opened the door, stepped inside and pushed it shut behind her. The latched hadn't even clicked into place when Zac shoved his way into the room. In a move so quick she didn't see it coming or going, he had the door closed and Freddie trapped between his hard body and the wall.

Air rushed through her lips a second before he took her mouth in a kiss that demanded full surrender. He drove his fingers into her hair and gripped her head as though he were trying to stop her from escaping. But Freddie had no desire to get away. She sighed and the soft sound was swallowed by the groan that rumbled deep in Zac's throat.

"Can't keep my hands off you," he spoke against her mouth.

Freddie didn't bother to answer. She let her hands do the talking, unbuttoned his shirt and shoved her hands under the open sides to get at his hot flesh. With fingers that shook, she explored his back, the muscles hot and firm beneath her touch. He growled and drove his tongue deeper into her mouth, and when she slipped her fingertips beneath the waistband of his slacks, he rocked his hips into her, pressing his hard cock against her.

"God, you drive me fucking insane." He nipped at her bottom lip. Licked the sting away. "I need to taste you again."

Zac tugged at the thin straps of her dress. Pushed them off her shoulders and down her arms until the bodice crumpled around her waist. Like underwear, Freddie had gone without a bra.

"Fuck, you're gorgeous." He stared down at her for a heartbeat before he leaned down and buried his face between her breasts. "I love your tits."

His words vibrated over her skin and her already hard nipples tightened further. The straining tips throbbed with need as he scrapped his stubbled jaw over each one in turn. She let her head fall back and slapped her hands against the wall as a moan left her throat. "Zac."

ZAC PULLED his mouth away from the nipple he was about

to suck between his lips and stared at Red. "Shit." He laid his forehead on hers. "Don't talk."

Their laboured breathing echoed around them and his pulse pounded in his ears—his dick. He needed to think.

"Don't say a word. I need to think."

He watched through hooded eyes as her tits rose and fell on each ragged breath she took. Her puckered nipples were tempting him beyond reason and he clenched his jaw, grinding his back teeth in an effort to thwart the need racing through him.

"You fuck with my head." He closed his eyes in the hope of clearing the lust fog weaving its way through his brain. "I can't think when you talk."

"Ah, Zac." Her warm breath bathed his mouth, making his lips twitch and his gut clench. "I'm not talking."

Zac could hear the humor in her voice. Knew if he opened his eyes, he'd see a smile on her kiss-swollen mouth. "Shh...no more talking."

Red laughed. A deliciously sexy chuckle that had his eyes opening and his brain thinking one thought. He had to taste that happy sound. The growl that rumbled in his chest was the only warning either of them had before he took her mouth once more.

A sexy little whimper tripped off her tongue onto his and she dug her hands into his back, urging him closer. He bucked his hips and ground his cock against the softness of her belly in a rhythmic thrust that had his balls aching and tucking up into his groin.

Dampness coated the head of his cock and Zac knew if he didn't stop now, he'd be covered in come instead of pre-come before long. With great difficulty, he tore his mouth from Red's.

"I..." Zac had no idea what he wanted to say. His gaze met hers. The sparkling blue depths of her eyes filled with a million promises of pleasure held his, and he couldn't deny either of them anymore. "I want you. Now."

Her eyes dilated further as she dragged her tongue along her bottom lip. "Yes."

Zac didn't waste any time getting her the rest of the way out of her dress. He found the small zipper in back and tugged it open before working the material over her hips and down her thighs. When the blue silk swirled around her feet, he discovered something that almost made him swallow his tongue.

She wasn't wearing any underwear.

No bra. No undies.

Naked.

And she'd been that way beneath her sexy-as-hell dress all day. He closed his eyes on a groan. "You're killing me, Red."

"And you love every fucking second of it."

Zac opened his eyes and zeroed in on her mouth. "You like knowing you get to me?"

She smiled the smile of a woman who knew her power over a man. "Fuck, yes."

He traced a fingertip across her lips. "You have a dirty mouth."

Her smile grew wider. "I seem to recall you like my dirty mouth."

"I prefer it when it's occupied with dirty things other than talking."

Red pressed her hand to his chest and slowly dragged her fingers down his torso, raking her nails over his skin. "What kind of things?"

Zac sucked in a breath and held it. Anticipation thrummed through his veins as he waited for her to reach his cock.

"Are they *hard* things?" she asked as she plastered her delicate hand over the bulge in his pants.

"Yes," he hissed through his teeth when she squeezed him.

"Should I get dirty now?"

She stroked him. Up and down. Up and down. Her hand was driving him insane. Add in the memories of her lush mouth wrapped around his cock... "Fuck, yes."

In a flash, she was on her knees, ripping at the opening of his pants. She made a humming noise that buzzed through him, lighting sparks in his veins and turning his whole body into a tinderbox just waiting for ignition.

The second she freed his cock, her mouth engulfed him. Hot. Wet. Soft. Red's mouth sucked him in, bringing him to his toes as a climax roared through him. He shook. Shuddered so violently that his teeth rattled in his head. And spilled everything he had in the back of her throat.

"Jesus. Fucking. Christ." Zac threw his hands out, grabbed the wall and barely kept his legs under him. He'd never come so hard and so fast in his life. "Fuck. Are you trying to kill me," he panted.

Red was still on her knees. Still lapping at his cock. His hard cock. And as soon as he caught his breath—could think over the roaring in his ears, see through the haze that blurred his vision—he was going to throw her on the bed and fuck her brains out.

2

FREDDIE LEANED back on her heels and looked up Zac's body. His heavy cock jutted out of his open pants, the thick shaft glistening with her saliva and looking ready to go in spite of the fact she'd just sucked it dry.

Damn, the man had stamina.

She couldn't help the little grin that tickled her lips as she admired the sculptured chest that sawed in and out on harsh breaths he still hadn't gotten under control.

The smirk on her mouth grew. His shirt hung open, his pants gaped and he looked well and truly rumpled. She loved knowing she'd stripped him of his restraint. He was always so put together, so calm, that watching him lose it gave her a sexual thrill she never expected. She'd never wanted to ruffle someone's feathers more.

Out of control looked good on Zac. Damn good.

She leaned over and swiped her tongue across the head of his cock where the slit wept more of the tasty treat she'd just consumed. "Mmm..."

"Don't."

The one word was a growl, and Freddie shivered as the vibration rolled over her. "Don't what?"

"Don't talk." He reached down and slid his hands under her arms. He brought her to her feet and pulled her close until their noses touched. "No more talking."

He leaned around her and flicked the lock. The small snick echoed in the room like the clang of a jail-cell door. But it wasn't fear that skittered down her spine. She closed her eyes and savoured the heat radiating off him. His scent surrounded her—filled her. Summer. He smelled like sunshine, freshly mown grass and the sea.

Her eyes flew open when he picked her up and took the few steps to the bed. "One word answer only," he growled.

Freddie blinked. "What?"

"Are you on the pill?"

Her mind whirled. She was, but she didn't have unprotected sex.

"It's not a hard question. Yes or no," he demanded.

She licked her lips. Opened her mouth to answer, but he cut her off.

"I'm clean. Haven't been with anyone since last year. Except you. And I *never* screw without a condom." Zac's hazel eyes dilated. "You, I want bare."

Freddie knew she could trust him—take him at his word—and she'd be lying if she didn't admit to the same desire. She wanted to feel him skin on skin. Wanted to feel him flood her insides with his come. Besides, she'd swallowed him twice now. The safe-sex ship had already sailed.

"Yes or no," he ground out through clenched teeth.

"Yes—"

He spun her around and pushed her face-down on the bed. She managed to do no more than turn her head to the side before he was on top of her, pushing her legs apart with his as he shoved his hips between her thighs and made room for his cock in the slick folds of her pussy.

She felt his heat before his skin pressed against hers. "No more talking," he murmured in her ear before nipping at her lobe and sending a shaft of lust through her core.

Her back arched of its own volition, her hips pushing up and opening her to him. "Please."

"Shh...no talking, remember." Zac licked the shell of her ear —her neck. "Just feel. Feel every inch of me as I take you this first time."

He pressed forward. Parting her in a slow, steady pace that just about drove her out of her mind. She tried to lift—push backwards—but he held her pinned to the bed and took his time.

"God, you're tight. Hot. Wet," he breathed in her ear, the words sending shivers over her skin.

Freddie moaned as he stretched her. Relaxed her pelvis in an effort to speed up his penetration.

Zac chuckled in her ear. "Greedy girl."

He rocked his hips, thrust just that little bit deeper, and she gasped around a moan. "Zac. Please," she pleaded.

"Not yet."

Nothing she did swayed him. He continued to enter her slowly. It felt like an eternity before he filled her—before the hot press of his pubic bone against her arse signified she'd taken all of him. She whimpered with the wave of pleasure that washed over her.

"Damn. This isn't going to go the way I want."

Freddie had no idea what Zac meant. But she didn't care when he gripped her hips in his big hands and pulled them both to their knees. He pressed a hand between her shoulder blades to keep her head down.

"Stay like that," he growled.

She wasn't about to argue. Not when he was pulling out and slamming back in over and over again. Each withdrawal dragged his hard flesh against her sensitive inner walls. Each plunge forward rammed his cockhead into the spot high inside her body that fed and twisted her need until nothing else mattered but the climax waiting to break.

ZAC STARED down at the woman spread out before him. She was the sexiest thing he'd ever laid his eyes on. Her hair was tussled about her head, the long strands covering the pillow where he'd swept it away from her face. The arch of her back pushed her hips up and gave him the perfect view of her gorgeous arse. He palmed her cheeks, plumped them with his fingers before pulling them apart to get a good look at her cunt taking his cock.

"Fuck." He shuddered. "Do you have any idea how hot you look impaled on my cock?"

She grunted as he rammed into her harder.

He brushed a thumb over the pucker of her anus. "Ever taken it in the arse, Red?"

Zac wasn't sure if the sound she made was a yes or no.

"Doesn't matter. When I'm done fucking your cunt, I'm fucking this tight arse." He pressed harder against the firm ring of muscle until it opened. "Oh, yeah. I'm definitely fucking you here next."

A moan broke in her throat when he pushed his thumb deeper. She was so hot and tight around him that he knew screwing her arse would be the best he'd ever had, and he couldn't stop his body's response to the thought of fucking her there. He drove his cock into her cunt as he buried his thumb to the hilt.

Red screamed.

Her orgasm tore through her, taking them both by storm. Zac gripped her arse, his thumb imbedded, while he pounded his cock into her. The walls of her cunt milked him as they clenched and released with wave after wave of her climax. As the last of her contractions ebbed, he plunged deep and let himself go.

He came.

Hard.

Harder than he had down her throat only minutes ago.

Shaking and sweating, he leaned forward and covered her. His chest heaved with each breath his labouring lungs pulled in and his head throbbed—the one on his shoulders and the one between his legs.

Zac expected his cock to deflate. He'd blown his load twice, and by rights he should be done for. But he wasn't. His prick was still rock hard and he knew he'd stay that way for hours yet. Red did that to him. Made him crave like he never had.

She collapsed beneath him and he rolled to the side, taking her with him and keeping his cock buried in her still-quivering cunt. He eased his thumb out of her and smiled at the moan of pleasure that spilled over her lips.

"So, dirty girl, you gonna answer me now?" he asked against her neck.

"Huh?"

"Have you ever let a guy fuck your arse?"

She turned her head and glanced over her shoulder at him. "Does it matter?"

From this angle, he couldn't read her face well, and really, it shouldn't matter. But it did. He wanted to claim some part of her no one else ever had. "Yes or no?"

The sigh that left her as she turned away had Zac's gut clenching. "No," she whispered.

A rush of air left his chest. "Good. I'll be the first." *The only.*

Zac wasn't dumb enough to voice those last two words. The ones before had made her stiffen in his arms as it was. He dropped a kiss on her shoulder before loosening his grip and slowly pulling away from her. Her cunt clamped down on his cock as he slid out of her and he had to fight the urge to drive himself back in again.

"Let's take a shower."

Before she could argue, he hauled her off the bed and into his arms. He strode across the room to the en suite and straight into the open shower stall.

"Are you going to make a habit of carrying me around," Red murmured.

He grinned. "You do feel good in my arms." Zac positioned them so they wouldn't be blasted with cold water.

She leaned her head back and opened slumberous eyes. "Don't get used to it."

"Why not?" he asked as he flicked the lever for the shower.

Red studied him through lowered lashes and Zac tried not to squirm under her scrutiny. She shook her head.

"What?"

"Mind-blowing sex doesn't give you the keys to the city."

"What's that supposed to mean?" He walked them under the warm water.

"No more talking." She leaned in and slanted her mouth over his. Wiggling in his arms, she managed to rub her erect nipples against his chest and send his need back into high gear.

Zac rearranged her so her arms were wrapped around his neck and her legs around his waist. He raised her, dragged her damp cunt along his cock and then onto his belly. "Take me inside you," he growled into her mouth.

For a second, he thought she'd deny him—them—but then

she arched her back, reached behind her with one arm and grabbed his cock in her fist. With her eyes on his, Red lined their bodies up and slowly took him in.

His eyes crossed and a moan rumbled deep in his belly as her slick heat swallowed his straining length. She took him to the root. Her tight walls a wet sheath that licked along his shaft, sending aching need into his balls.

"Feels so fucking good." She tangled her fingers in his hair, gripped and tugged, delivering a sensual thrill Zac hadn't encountered before.

Red moaned as she rolled her pelvis, sliding his cock through those slick walls and driving him out of his mind. She did something with her internal muscles, something that undulated her soft tissues in a wet caress that coiled the tension building in his groin tighter. Higher.

Her mouth met his in a hungry kiss. She thrust her tongue between his lips and plundered. He'd taken her before. Taken her mouth by storm, and it seemed she was intent on returning the favour. But she didn't know how close he was to breaking. How close he was to giving in to the all-consuming compulsion to claim her as his.

"Please." Her desperate plea tangled with his tongue and sent him over.

Zac spun around and slammed her against the shower wall. His eyes went blind, the need flashing through him obliterating all but the feel of Red wrapped around him—against him. He powered his hips, ramming his cock into the sweet heaven she offered. She fought as hard as he did, her body straining against his as they sought relief together.

"Harder."

Her breath burst in hot pants against his neck where she buried her face.

"Faster."

"Fuck." He drove into her, impaled her again and again.

"More."

Zac gripped her hips, his hold punishing enough to bruise, but he couldn't stop the out-of-control desperation slicing through him with razor-sharp edges.

"Harder, dammit." Red sank her teeth into the slope of his neck and Zac wondered how he'd ever survive this.

Survive her.

Lost in sensation—in the burning fire of their mutual need—he rode her harder than he ever dreamed possible.

"Yes." The cry tore from Red's lips as her climax hit, and Zac could do nothing except follow her into bliss.

FREDDIE LAY in the pre-dawn light wondering what the hell to do now. Zac was sprawled on the bed beside her, his soft snoring reminding her she wasn't alone. She'd given in without thought. Regardless of how he'd treated her in recent months, how much she'd hated his behaviour, all it had taken was one kiss and she'd been his for the taking.

She wouldn't delude herself into thinking this was more than it appeared. Hot sex between two consenting—unattached—adults. At least for him it was. And she certainly wasn't going to read anything into the fact he'd been without female companionship since their last hot-and-heavy session.

Noise and movement filtered into the room through the locked door and Freddie knew she had to get up. West and Kelsey would be leaving soon, and the last thing she wanted to do was have West find her in bed with his best friend. Her brother was sure to explode over her and Zac sleeping together, and she wasn't ready to deal with him yet. Not until she'd gotten this thing with Zac sorted out.

She didn't think Zac would be too thrilled for them to be found in bed either.

With as much stealth as she could manage, she slipped off the side of the bed and padded into the bathroom. A wall of memories slammed into her as she cleared the doorway. Already achy and stiff from the athletic aspect of their night, she didn't need the added reminder and tried to push the images out of her head as she got in the shower.

She could still smell him—smell them—on her skin, and while she wanted to be able to savour their night, Freddie knew she needed to move on.

He'd given her the fuck of her life. What wasn't sore tingled with awareness, and she couldn't help but shiver as the warm water ran over her hypersensitive skin. It would be a long time before she forgot about how amazing Zac was in bed. And out of it.

Shit. Who was she kidding? There'd be no forgetting. Ever.

Freddie just had to hope she didn't turn into one of those mooning, clingy females she despised so much. She'd never been one before, but with Zac all her usual traits seem to have taken a hike. The man had her checking her phone and searching a crowd for a glimpse of his handsome face.

Damn. She had it bad, and the sinking realisation that last night would only amplify her infatuation with her brother's best friend settled over her. Closing her eyes, Freddie took a deep breath and blew it out through her mouth.

God. She was such a fool.

It didn't matter how often she told herself sex was sex. With Zac, there was no such thing. At least for her there wasn't. Because she'd already had feelings for him. He'd been part of her life for as long as she could remember, and while she couldn't say she'd never thought of him in a sexual sense, she couldn't say those vague notions had ever strung her nerves taut the way they did now.

And now she had memories—Technicolor details—to add to her obscure fantasies. It definitely didn't help that reality far outstripped anything her imagination could have conjured up. With a groan, Freddie ducked her head under the shower and hoped the pounding spray would drown out her chaotic thoughts.

She could deal with the Zac issue once she was home and away from the temptation that lay spread out in all his naked glory in the next room. With a little distance—some time—Freddie was sure she'd be able to get a rational perspective of the whole thing. Then again, for all she knew, Zac would go back to ignoring her.

A sharp pain lanced her chest at the thought of being shoved aside again. That, more than anything else, told her how deep in trouble she was. Zac had always been in her heart, and now he'd stamped his brand all over her body—inside her body.

"Morning, gorgeous." Zac slid his arms around her waist.

"Argh!"

"Sorry." He nuzzled the back of her neck, pushing the wet strands of hair aside with his nose. "I thought you heard me open the door."

She'd been so deep in thought she'd barely registered the water hitting the tiled floor, never mind the bathroom door opening. "No."

"You shouldn't be surprised. Who else would be climbing into the shower with you?" he murmured against her ear.

Who else indeed. "I thought you were still asleep."

He nudged his hips forward, sliding the hard ridge of his cock along the crease of her arse. "As you can feel, I'm wide awake."

The hot slide of his cock on her sensitive skin sent a

shudder through her, and Freddie knew if he pushed for more, she wouldn't be able to say no. A small whimper curled in the back of her throat, and she wasn't sure if it was a sound of frustration, need or surrender.

Zac's hands roamed up her torso until he cupped her heavy breasts in his palms. She arched her back and pressed the puckered tips deeper into his caress. His fingers strummed her nipples, brushed and tweaked and twisted until the sounds emanating from her throat were definitely need.

"I want you again," he said in her ear.

God help her. She couldn't deny herself another taste of the pleasure Zac could give her. "Yes."

3

ZAC LEANED against the wall and tried to catch his breath. Red was boneless in his arms, and he had to admit he loved holding her this way—all soft and satisfied after he'd taken them both on a hot, hard ride. He knew he had a grin on his face. One that probably made him look like a besotted fool, but he didn't care.

All he cared about was that he had Red in his arms again. When he'd woken to find himself alone, he couldn't say what emotion had blindsided him more. The gut-wrenching thought of her sneaking out on him or the slashing disappointment of not seeing her face the second he opened his eyes.

He wasn't stupid. He knew he was in way deeper than he should be at this stage of the game, but that didn't stop him from thinking things he'd never thought about with any other woman. Not even in a vague the-woman-I'll-spend-my-life-with way. No one had inspired the kind of future plans he was suddenly entertaining about Red.

"I need to get out."

Zac grunted in reply.

"West will be up soon."

Shit. Nothing like the mental image of his pissed-off best friend staring him down to obliterate the contentment flooding his mind—to vapourise any happy thoughts woven around the woman in his arms. "What time do they leave?"

"A car is picking them up at seven."

"Plenty of time."

"Not if you're going to sneak out of the house without anyone seeing you." She pushed out of his arms and reached over to turn off the water.

Red mumbled something under her breath. Something that sounded suspiciously like she didn't need to deal with another annoying male first thing in the morning. Zac wanted to call her on it. Wanted to know what about him annoyed her. Especially when her face was still flushed from the orgasm he'd just given her. But before he could utter a word, she'd wrapped a towel around herself and left him alone in the steam-filled bathroom.

"Shit." He snatched up a towel from the pile on the counter and rubbed himself dry.

When he entered the bedroom, Red was already dressed in a pair of shorts and T-shirt. She obviously hadn't wasted any time covering up. When she turned to face him, he noticed she'd not only donned the clothes to hide behind. She'd managed to mask her emotions as well.

Those crystal-blue eyes held no clue to what she was thinking—what she was feeling—and Zac felt the loss of that doorway to the inner workings of her mind like a kick to the gut.

"I'll go out and make sure the coast is clear while you get dressed." She headed for the door. With her hand on the knob, she glanced over her shoulder. "Don't come out until I tell you it's okay."

She left him standing in the middle of the room with a multitude of emotions burning through him. The one he chose to focus on was the anger. She'd dismissed him as though they hadn't spent the night tearing up the sheets. As though he hadn't been buried inside her tight body no more than ten minutes ago.

He let the head of steam build while he searched for last night's clothes. The last thing he wanted to do was have a confrontation with West, but he wanted to have it out with Red before she got farther away from him. She was pulling away, and he didn't like it. Not one little bit. Dressed, he stormed across the room and threw the door open.

And came face-to-face with his best friend.

Neither of them spoke. Both were too stunned to utter a word until West looked over Zac's shoulder into the room and saw the disheveled bedding.

"You fucking son of bitch!"

Zac didn't have time to dodge the punch and probably wouldn't have if he'd seen it coming. He figured West deserved one shot at him. But only one. He kept his feet when he took the hit and brought his hand to his throbbing jaw. "That's your free one."

"West!" Kelsey grabbed on to her husband's arm. "What the hell is wrong with you?"

"Let me go." West yanked his arm from Kelsey's hold. "I'm not done yet."

"Yes, you are." Kelsey planted herself in front of West, her hands on his chest.

Zac knew his friend could simply move his wife aside if he really wanted to and braced himself for the next blow. He wouldn't be taking this one on the chin.

"Kels. Move out of my way," West ground out through his clenched jaw.

"No." Kelsey tried to move her husband back without luck. "You need to calm down."

"Calm down?" West nodded his head in Zac's direction. "This fucker messed with something he shouldn't have. I know you distracted me last night, but there's no getting around it this morning."

"West."

As one, the three of them turned to see Red standing with her feet apart, hands on her hips and a scowl on her face. Zac thought it was poor form to note how sexy she looked all riled up, but he was a guy with a serious attraction and he couldn't ignore the hot chick staring down her six-foot-plus brother without fear. He grinned. The glare she threw his way soon had him rethinking his smile.

"You." Red pointed at him. "Go home."

Zac took a half-step back. Her words caused more damage to his equilibrium than her brother's physical blow had. "What?"

"Go home. I can't deal with both of you right now." She turned back to West and Zac's insides scraped raw at the dismissal. "Are you ready to go? The car will be here in fifteen minutes."

"I'm not going anywhere with this fucker hanging around." West crossed his arms over his chest, and if Zac hadn't spent most of his life wrestling with the guy, he might actually be intimidated by his friend's aggressive stance.

"Oh for God's sake." Red threw her hands in the air. "Fine. Beat the shit out of him. It won't change a damn thing. What's done is done."

Zac watched as Red stalked down the hallway and out of sight. He turned back to West. "I—"

"Don't say it." West dragged a hand down his face. "I don't

want to hear anything you have to say unless it's 'I didn't touch her'."

Zac pulled his lips between his teeth and held his best friend's gaze.

"Well, fuck."

For a moment, West glared at him in a similar expression to his sister's and Zac marvelled at how the look worried him less than the one Red had given him. Then his friend of twenty-three years—the man who knew all his secrets bar one—shook his head and walked away, leaving him alone with Kelsey.

Kelsey put a hand on Zac's arm. "I'll talk to him."

"Why? He has every right to be pissed, Kelsey."

"No, he doesn't. Freddie is a grown woman and free to see whoever she chooses. West needs to remember she's no longer the fragile teenager in need of his protection."

"She's still his little sister. And I'm his best friend." Zac glanced in the direction West had gone. "At least I was."

Funny how the thought of losing West's friendship didn't cut him as deep as Red walking away from him did.

"HAVE A GREAT TIME," Freddie called out as she finally waved her brother and sister-in-law off.

They were leaving thirty minutes later than planned, but thankfully, there was still plenty of time for them to make their flight. It had taken both her and Kelsey's considerable effort to convince West he should go on their honeymoon as planned. He seemed determined to hunt down Zac and, in his words, "Teach him what it means to be a friend."

A reluctant smile tugged at her mouth. West might be on the overprotective side, but his intentions were pure. He loved her and didn't want to see her hurt. She was just sorry it was his best friend he wanted to kill. With a sigh, she turned back to the house and found herself facing the very man West wanted to find, the one she'd sent home an hour ago.

"What are you still doing here?"

He cocked one eyebrow.

Long seconds passed while she waited for an answer. Zac didn't budge. He just stared at her with turbulent multi-coloured eyes, and for the life of her, Freddie couldn't read anything in his gaze.

"God save me from stubborn men." She marched past him and into the house.

Freddie didn't bother to close the door behind her. Zac would just open it again. When he trailed her inside, she pretended he wasn't there and went about straightening up and checking everything was the way it should be before she had to lock up and return the key.

His hot gaze followed her everywhere. There was no point looking at him. She'd only end up giving in to the arousal thrumming in her veins. Even being pissed off that Zac hadn't left like she'd asked didn't dampen her desire. Her body was primed and ready to tangle with him again.

She couldn't understand the sudden intensity with which she craved him. He'd barely blipped her attraction metre a year ago. Now she couldn't think about him without getting hot and bothered, and that alone was enough to irritate her beyond reason. Add in the scene with her brother...

Her gaze darted across the room, searching Zac out and finding him with a telling quickness. His jaw was red and the shadow of a bruise was already forming. "Does it hurt?"

"Not as much as you ordering me to leave before we had a chance to talk." He stayed where he was, but she could see the effort it took for him to remain there—his hands were fisted at his sides and held a tautness that appeared on the verge of snapping. "I didn't like being dismissed, Red."

"Why do you keep calling me that?"

His eyelids lowered and one corner of his mouth kicked up. "To remind myself to stay away from you."

"Stay away?" Freddie's brows furrowed. "I don't get it."

"Red as in danger zone. Keep clear." He shrugged. "I started thinking of you as Red after I touched you the first time."

What the fuck? "Why?"

"Why what?"

"Why would you need to stay away from me?" Freddie held her breath. She wasn't sure what it was she feared, but there was no denying the streak of anxiety winding its way through her middle, drawing tighter and tighter.

"I shouldn't have touched you. Shouldn't *want* to touch you."

"Why not? You're not seeing anyone. *I'm* not seeing anyone. What's the problem?"

"You're West's sister," Zac growled.

She stumbled back a step. Her mouth opened but no words formed on her tongue.

"My best friend's *little sister!*"

Freddie didn't care for the emphasis on little sister. She couldn't believe that he'd been thinking any type of sisterly thoughts last night or when they'd hooked up months ago. There was no stopping the twisted laughter that burst from her mouth. "Sister? You expect me to believe you were thinking like my brother when you stripped off my dress? When you threw me on the bed and shoved your cock inside me? When you fucked me against the wall in the shower? Twice!"

"Jesus." Zac scrubbed a hand down his face, flinching when he reached his bruised jaw. "I can't believe how dirty your mouth is."

"You're worried about my dirty mouth when you *told* me

you want to fuck my arse?" She shook her head. "You know what? You're right. You shouldn't have touched me if all you see when you look at me is West's little sister."

Freddie spun on her heel and headed for the bedroom and her overnight bag. She had to get out of here. Get away from Zac before she did something like throw the expensive vase on the hall table at his head. "Little sister my arse." No man screwed a woman the way Zac had her and thought *sister*.

She ignored the brooding man behind her and collected her things. Bag in hand, she walked through the house checking all the windows and doors were shut and locked. Freddie led Zac out the front door without a word. She'd be damned if she'd be the first to speak. As far as she was concerned, the idiot could take a long walk off a short pier.

Fuming, she slung her suitcase into the backseat of her car and climbed behind the wheel. She slammed the door and fired the engine with a roar. Mindful of her agitated mood and the fact she was sitting in what amounted to a deadly weapon, Freddie sucked in a breath and tried for calm.

Convinced she wouldn't run the frustrating man over—on purpose or by accident—Freddie put the car in gear and reversed out of the driveway. She continued to mumble and curse him under her breath until she pulled up at the rental office and discovered he'd followed her.

Refusing to acknowledge him in any way, she got out of her car and went inside to return the keys.

Finding him waiting for her when she was done didn't give her a thrill like it would have at any time in the last six months. Instead, she felt suddenly drained of energy and in need of solitude.

Freddie knew she'd have to deal with Zac sooner or later, but right now she didn't have the strength to handle her emotions, never mind his. With a sigh, she got back in her car and headed home.

She only hoped he'd take the hint and leave her alone when she got there.

ZAC KNEW he'd blown it. He wasn't sure where it had gone wrong other than the obvious arrival of West at the bedroom door. What he did know was that he had to fix it. Now.

Shame he didn't have the first clue of where to start.

He leaned his head back against the car seat and stared through the windshield at Red's house. He'd followed her home over an hour ago with the intention of getting out and talking to her when they got here, but one look at her face and Zac had known nothing he said would make things right.

So he'd turned off the engine and sat brooding while she'd gone inside without him. Zac had gone over and over this morning until he couldn't think anymore. If he could just get her in his arms, he knew he could convince her to stay there.

Maybe.

There'd been something in her gaze back at the house when she'd turned away that last time that sat in his chest like a bad case of heartburn.

Zac rubbed the spot on his chest that burned hottest. His phone buzzed beside him but he didn't bother picking it up. Coop had been calling and texting for the last hour. He figured either West or Kelsey had rung his brother, and Zac wasn't in the mood to talk to anyone except Red.

And before he could do that, he needed to work out what to say.

His phone rang out twice more and he was reaching over to turn it off when Red's front door opened. She stood in the doorway, phone in her hand. He could see she was tapping away at the screen and then his phone rang again.

Glancing over at the phone, he saw Red's name and quickly grabbed it and hit answer. "Hello."

"Go home, Zac." She sounded so tired.

He sighed. "We need to talk."

"No. No more talking. Not now."

Zac debated getting out of the car, but her next words stopped him.

"Please, Zac," she pleaded. "Just go home."

He closed his eyes. It was the please—the shaky way she'd said it—that did him in. "Okay. But first tell me when we'll talk."

Zac was sure his heart didn't beat for the eternity he waited for Red to answer him. He definitely didn't take a breath.

"I don't know. I need to think."

"Tomorrow?" Zac wanted to say tonight but didn't want to push her away any farther than he already had. He could feel her backing away from him—from what they'd shared—and cold fear slid down his spine. "At least send me a text to let me know you're okay."

Her heavy sigh filled the phone line. "Sure."

"And you'll ring if you need anything?"

The laughter that met his ear held no humour. "What could I possibly need, Zac?"

Me.

He didn't say it, but he felt it in every part of him. And that was the moment he realised Red wasn't the only one who needed time. Because no matter what his body wanted. No matter that he'd gladly walk inside her house and take her again, he still couldn't get past the fact she was his best friend's little sister.

4

"ARGH." Freddie tossed her phone on the sofa. "Men are idiots."

Not only had her stupid brother called her from the airport, but he also contacted Coop and sent him around to check on her. Although, to give Cooper credit, he'd told her it wasn't *her* he was checking on exactly. He was looking for Zac.

She was so worked up over her brother's interference that she almost lied about seeing Zac. But in the end, Freddie had given Coop what little info she could.

After telling Zac to go home, she'd come inside so she didn't have to watch him leave. She knew it was best for both of them to take a step back, but part of Freddie—a big part—was afraid she'd stop him from going if she saw him leave. So she'd avoided all windows for a good twenty minutes.

And when she'd finally given in to the need to find out if he'd done as she'd asked, the street in front of her house was empty.

Freddie had to admit she hadn't liked the hollowness that filled her chest. She shouldn't have been disappointed to see

Zac gone—she'd asked him to leave after all—except there was that little piece inside her that crumbled anyway. He'd given up.

She glanced at her phone.

He hadn't called or sent a text either. Everyone else—including her mother—had. But not Zac. He'd done as she asked and she wished he hadn't. She really did need to get a handle on her emotions or she'd never work out what to do about them.

And to top it off, now she had to deal with Pierce Taylor. The personal trainer she occasionally worked with hadn't taken no for an answer when she'd told him she couldn't consult about one of his clients today. Mind you, the man they were supposed to discuss did have serious health issues that required not just the exercise program Pierce would put together for him. Any exercise affected blood sugar levels, and as a recently diagnosed diabetic, Mr. Turner needed to be sure he was managing his diet around the times he worked out.

At least she'd managed to convince Pierce to meet her at the office. The idea of meeting at a café hadn't sat right with her and only brought home the fact she needed to set him straight. His overtures had been subtle enough that Freddie had questioned whether or not he was coming on to her. Until today. Ending their call with, "See you soon, sweetheart," with a syrupy tone to his voice had set off warning bells in her head.

Loud ones.

Freddie went into the spare bedroom she used as a home office and grabbed her laptop. She'd worked with a few diabetics in the past and it would be simple to tweak one of those existing meal plans to suit Mr. Turner. If she was lucky, she could deal with Pierce and be heading home again in less than an hour.

The beauty of having her own business was being able to

house it wherever she wanted, and Freddie loved the little cottage she'd bought on the quiet street of Manly. It was close to the beach and shops, and yet traffic—pedestrian and vehicular—was minimal. It also allowed her to set up her office like a home.

Being able to show her clients how to prepare a nutritionally balanced meal was just as important as handing out meal plans, recipes and shopping lists. It was also simpler and easier to demonstrate how to make one of her nutrient-supplementing smoothies than to try to explain how.

Sunday afternoon traffic was light, and Freddie pulled into the driveway of her office within twenty minutes of leaving home. She'd spent the entire drive replaying everything that had happened with Zac since he'd pushed his way into her room last night.

She could have another twenty days to think about it and still not be any closer to knowing what to do.

With a sigh, Freddie turned off the engine and opened the door. Climbing out of the car, she surveyed the yard. The service she hired to look after the gardens had done a great job yesterday. Her one stipulation was for the place to look lived in—just like every other house on the quiet residential street.

Freddie wanted her clients to feel comfortable and relaxed when they came to see her. A lot of them were making dietary changes due to poor health or illness, like Mr. Turner, and she knew all too well how either of those could affect a person.

Memories of her own struggle with anorexia filled her head. A shudder rattled through her. She pushed the bad thoughts aside and pulled up the good ones. The ones of the woman who'd helped Freddie get control of her chaotic mind and her eating. Janice had not only saved her from herself, but also inspired her to help others who were dealing with food issues. Hence Freddie acquiring degrees in nutrition and psychology.

With a smile on her face, Freddie walked to the front door. She slipped her key into the lock and turned it. The beep of the alarm system started the second she opened the door and she quickly punched in the code to deactivate it. Having the security company turn up on her doorstep would be one more disaster this weekend didn't need.

Cool and quiet, the air held a trace of the flowers she'd set on the entryway table. She needed to remember to pick up some more on the way to work in the morning. Moving deeper into the house, Freddie headed for the kitchen and her blender. A nice energy-boosting smoothie was just the thing to get her through the next hour or so.

She'd barely pulled the ingredients from the fridge when a commotion at the front door drew her into the hallway. What greeted her left her speechless and frozen to the spot for a second. But when Pierce pulled his arm back—fist clenched— she sprang into motion.

"Zac!"

PAIN RADIATED across Zac's face and into his skull. Blood burst from his nose. Ran into his mouth and down his chin. Damn. That was the second time today he hadn't seen a punch coming. He had no idea who the meathead that held him by the shirt was or where he'd come from, but Zac was paying attention now.

Using a move he'd learned from years of wrestling with his brothers, Zac dislodged the guy's arms from where he gripped Zac's shirt and took two steps back. He rolled to the balls of his feet and got ready for a second attack.

Only it never came because, before either he or the meathead could move another inch, Red came charging out the door like she'd been fired from a cannon.

"Zac. Oh my God." She reached his side and cupped her hands on his cheeks. "Hold still."

"What the hell?" Meathead asked.

Red glanced over at the muscle-bound punch thrower. "That's my question."

"He was hanging around your door. Looking inside."

"I was about to knock," Zac mumbled, the words muffled in his ears like he spoke under water, and even those softly spoken words sent pain lancing through his head.

"We need to get you a towel. Stop the bleeding. Do I need to take you to the hospital? Do you think it's broken?" Red rambled.

"Nah, not broken." Zac brought his hand up and pinched the bridge of his nose between his thumb and index finger, applying the necessary pressure to stop the flow of blood. "Fucking hurts like a bitch though."

"C'mon." Red took her hands away and turned to the guy who'd nailed him. "What the hell were you thinking, Pierce?"

Pierce? Who the fuck was Pierce?

"I thought he was going to attack you." The meathead —*Pierce*—crossed his behemoth arms over his equally huge barrel chest.

"From the front step?" Zac asked, genuinely confused because he hadn't hung back waiting at all. He'd gotten straight out of his car and walked to the front door.

Red shook her head and turned back to Zac. "C'mon. Let's get you cleaned up."

"Pain meds would be good too." Zac's head throbbed. Thanks to West and this guy, he had a blinding headache, and no doubt his face would be black and blue come morning.

Good thing he didn't have any pressing court cases this week. He could work from home if he needed to.

"I'm sure I've got something. If not, Pierce can go to the shop and get some seeing how he's the one who did the damage." Red led him into the house.

"Hey."

Zac winced. Pierce was right behind him so the guy's voice not only echoed off the walls, it bounced around the inside of Zac's head.

Red threw a daggered look at the guy but didn't say anything.

She took them through the house to the kitchen. Zac was surprised by what he saw. He knew from West that she'd set up her consultation rooms in a house, but he'd never been here. He had to admit, he was impressed by what he'd seen so far. When she pointed to a stool in front of a long counter, he took a seat.

The second he sat, Zac lowered his forehead to the cool countertop. He wouldn't admit it to anyone, but he couldn't deny he was a little wobbly on his feet right now. Between the pounding in his head and the blood still trickling from his nose, it was a wonder he'd made it this far.

"Here." Red smoothed her hand down his back. "Press this to your nose and you need to sit up straight, Zac."

He knew she was right. He'd had enough bloody noses in his lifetime to know what to do, but the urge to lay his head down and forget everything that had gone on in the last twelve or so hours since she'd come in his arms the last time was too much to deny. "Give me a sec."

"No." She tugged on his hair lightly, but it still shot a shaft of agony from the base of his skull to his eye sockets. "Stop bleeding then lie down."

"Bossy," Zac whispered.

"Better bossy than you bleeding to death all over my

counter." She stood behind him, her chest to his back, and helped him upright. "Lean back if you need to."

Zac wanted to lean against her. Not that he needed to. He might be a little woozy, but he wasn't that incapacitated that he couldn't sit up. "I'm good."

"Don't be a hero." Red pressed the cool damp towel into his hand. "Press this to your nose."

"Like I said. Bossy."

"Bossy over bleeding preferred."

"Freddie, he's obviously fine. He doesn't need you babying him."

Zac had forgotten the meathead was still there. "Who *is* this guy?" He didn't mean for the question to slip out, but his brain wasn't exactly firing on all cylinders at the moment.

"Who the fuck are *you*?" Pierce the meathead growled.

Zac stiffened, but the hand Red placed on his shoulder stopped him from getting up and punching the dickhead.

"Zac this is Pierce Taylor. I occasionally consult on his clients."

Zac was pleased by the way she introduced them. She was clearly stating what place each of them held in her life. Zac was a friend, while Pierce was a work associate. He grunted but didn't offer his hand.

"You know him?" Pierce asked, his gaze directed over Zac's right shoulder where Red stood behind him offering her support.

"Of course I know him. Why else would he be at my office on a Sunday?"

Why indeed. Zac couldn't stop the smirk from forming. Good thing he held the towel on his nose, it covered the whole bottom half of his face from view.

"I didn't realise you had a boyfriend," Pierce said, a frown pulling the corners of his mouth down.

Red moved closer to Zac's back, pressing her soft breasts into his shoulder blades. "And why would you know? It's not like we socialise outside of work, Pierce."

"Right. No. Right."

Zac almost felt sorry for the guy. He'd obviously had his sights set on Red.

"Speaking of work. We'll have to reschedule our consult. When are you seeing Mr. Turner? I've got a two o'clock half-hour slot Monday, but other than that I'm booked solid through the week," Red said.

"I was waiting to get the meal plan from you before making a time with him."

"Okay, then I'll see you tomorrow at two."

It was a clear dismissal. One just as obvious as when Red had directly told Zac to go home earlier today. Twice. He frowned.

"I..." Pierce's gaze bounced between Red and Zac. "Right. Okay. Well, sorry about..." He waved a hand towards Zac's face.

"Yeah." Zac wasn't going to let the guy off the hook completely. "Next time, you might want to think before you punch. Assault is a charge you don't want to be brought up on."

"Assault?" Meathead's face paled.

"Yep. Unprovoked too."

"But...I..."

Red squeezed Zac's shoulder, digging her nails into his skin through his shirt. "Zac's only winding you up. It's his lawyer sense of humour. Most of us don't find it anywhere near as amusing as he does."

"Lawyer?" Pierce's eyes bulged—more than his muscles—and Zac hid his grin behind the towel.

"As I said. He's joking. Right, Zac?" She dug her fingernails into him again.

"Yeah." He might have agreed verbally, but the guy would be an idiot not to read the warning Zac sent him with his eyes. Pierce might be muscle-bound but there were at least two brain cells rubbing together inside his thick head, because he took a step back.

"Sorry. Again. I'll see myself out." Then he was gone, leaving a heavy silence behind.

Neither of them spoke, and Zac was pleased that Red didn't move away either. He knew the bleeding had stopped and his vision was no longer blurred. The pounding in his head had eased a bit too. But even with all that, he couldn't deny himself the pleasure of touching her. Especially when she was the one doing the touching.

FREDDIE HAD NEVER BEEN MORE bewildered or confused as she was now. Even in the throes of her eating disorder, she'd had direction. It might have been destructive and life threatening, but she'd felt there'd been something to head towards—a goal. Right now, she didn't know whether to hold Zac closer or run a mile.

With a sigh, she moved to the side and propped her hip on the counter next to him. "How's the nose?"

"The bleeding has stopped."

"Do you want those pain pills?"

"That would be good." He pulled the towel away from his face and revealed a blood-smeared chin. "Got a bathroom I can clean up in?"

"Oh, sure. Down the hall." She pointed behind him. "You can't miss it. There's a sign on the door."

"Thanks. Be back in a second."

She watched him go. Wondered what the hell he was doing here. How he'd known she was here and whether either of them had a clue what they should do now. First things first though. They needed to take care of Zac's nose.

God. Twice today he'd taken a hit because of her. It was a wonder he hadn't bolted out of here by now. Pushing off the counter, Freddie looked around for her bag. She kept a travel pack of Panadol in there, and it would be simpler to grab those than open the first-aid kit in the supply room.

Zac would need a drink to take them. She knew he'd be fine with water, but with the thought of all that bruised tissue that his body would need to repair, not to mention the blood he needed to replace in mind, Freddie figured she'd put together a supplement-fortified smoothie. He'd probably refuse it—most people did—but she'd force it on him even if she had to blackmail him into drinking it.

The ingredients she'd laid out for herself earlier would suit what she had in mind. She'd add some protein powder as well as beetroot to oxygenate the blood and turmeric to fight inflammation and promote healing. She was ready to load everything into the blender when he returned.

"Oh, no. I'm not having one of those vile things," he protested, waving his hand at the counter in front of her.

"They're not vile and, yes, you are. Your body has taken a beating today. Literally. And you need to boost your system to help it repair the damage." Freddie dropped the banana, strawberries and spinach in the blender and snapped on the lid.

Zac frowned at her. "You can't make me."

She grinned. "Wanna bet?"

"Sure. What's the wager?"

"Dinner."

"Done."

"Drink it and I'll take my top off."

"What?" His mouth hung open.

"You heard me."

"Red," he growled.

"What?"

"I'm finding it hard to keep my hands off you while you've got your clothes on. Take any of them off, and I won't be able to control myself."

"You'll drink this?" She pointed at the blender she'd yet to turn on.

He blew out a breath and looked at the ceiling. "Jesus. I'm fucked."

Freddie laughed. "Not yet you're not, but you never know."

Before he—or she—could say another word, she flipped the switch.

5

ZAC SUCKED in a breath and stared at the ceiling. How did she do this to him? With little more than a smile and a promise, she had him tied in knots and struggling to keep control. The throbbing in his skull was no longer a problem. It was the pounding heat in his groin that almost brought him to his knees now.

"Red." He lowered his gaze to the woman who just might be the death of him.

She couldn't hear him over the whine of the blender, but her smile slipped a little when he took a step towards her. He waited until she switched off the machine and then took another step closer.

"You're playing with fire, you know that?" he asked as he shortened the distance between them once more.

Zac could see her hand trembling as she poured the thick pink liquid from the blender into a tall glass. "Here." She held it out to him. "Drink."

"And if I do, you'll take your top off?" He arched an eyebrow. She couldn't have been serious.

She nodded and caught the corner of her bottom lip between her teeth.

Fuck. His body tightened. His pulse raced with anticipation. And his gaze zeroed in on her mouth. The lush curves drove him wild. The things she could do with it...

He reached for the glass and their fingers brushed as he took it from her hand. Electricity sparked between them. There was no denying they had chemistry. It crackled to life whenever they were near, and Zac's grip on control grew thinner and thinner each time they were together.

Zac kept his eyes on hers as he brought the glass to his mouth. He couldn't say who was more surprised. Him, because he liked it, or Red, because he downed the whole thing in one go.

Leaning past her, Zac put the empty cup on the counter, making sure to slide his forearm across her breasts as he did. She shuddered but didn't step away. Her nipples beaded beneath her shirt, the buds poking against the fabric and making it clear she was turned on.

"Your turn." His voice was ragged, the strain he felt at having to hold himself back all too evident to his ears.

Red licked her lips and reached for the hem of her top. When she slid the material up her torso, Zac stopped breathing. When the delicate lace of her bra came into view, his mouth watered. And when she whipped the T-shirt over her head and dropped it on the floor at their feet, a sharp bolt of lust burned through him.

"Fuck." The word dragged through his throat like a razor blade.

He reached over and cupped her beasts in his palms. Felt her shiver and watched those tight little nipples grow harder.

"I need to touch you."

"You are touching me," she whispered on a shuddering breath.

"No." Zac used his thumbs to flick the clasp nestled between her cleavage open.

"Zac—"

"I have to. I can't help myself," he growled.

"We shouldn't." Her breath was choppy, the little gasps giving away the fact they should. Oh they definitely should. "We need to talk."

"Shh...no more talking."

"But—"

Zac lowered his mouth to her and spoke against her lips. "No. More. Talking."

He licked her lips. Pressed his tongue to the seam and urged her to open. A groan broke in his chest when she melted against him. His hands were trapped between them, her generous breasts crushed in his palms while he stroked her nipples with his thumbs.

Red opened her mouth and darted her hot tongue out to tangle with his. He swallowed the moan that tripped up her throat. Nibbled at her lips, her tongue, her lips. No matter how fast he went, how much he took, he couldn't get enough.

"Want you naked," he groaned.

"Yes. No." She pulled her mouth from his. "Not here."

Here? "What?"

"Not here."

Zac had no idea how it happened, but one second she was in his arms half naked and pliant, the next she was across the room and tugging her top back on.

"Here?"

"My work." Red wrapped her arms around her middle. "God. I think the front door is still open."

She rushed from the room, the echo of her flip-flops slapping on the floor trailing behind her. He dragged in a breath and tried to rein in his libido enough to make his brain work. Now that the heat of the kiss had dulled, Zac realised his face hurt like hell.

"Dammit." He was pretty sure his nose wasn't broken, but it was bloody close. He lowered his face into his hands. "Fucking son of a bitch."

"What? What's wrong?"

He hadn't heard Red come back, but she stood not two feet away, worry creasing her forehead.

"Nothing."

"Don't lie to me, Zac. Do you need to get your nose X-rayed?"

"No. But I could do with those pain pills."

She eyed him doubtfully. Finally, she said, "I'll grab the meds."

Zac breathed deeply. Lust still pulled at him, but he understood why Red had backed away. It would have taken less than a minute for them to be naked and writhing around on the floor. He figured the chances of them getting caught in a compromising position were low, but he had to respect her and her place of business.

He'd just wait until they got back to her house.

"Here." Red handed him two white pills and a glass of water.

He popped the tablets into his mouth and swallowed them dry. Taking a seat on one of the stools, he sipped at the cold water and watched her tidy up the kitchen. "So what do you want for dinner?"

Her head swiveled in his direction. "Dinner?"

"Yeah, that was the wager, remember?" He cocked his head. "Although I'm not sure which one of us actually won that bet." Zac grinned.

Red smiled. "I did."

"Oh, I don't know." Zac let his gaze drop to her chest before slowly bringing it back to meet hers. "Kinda feels like we both won."

Her cheeks flushed red and her eyes dilated. She licked her lips. "You should put an ice pack on that nose."

A change of subject. Nice. "I will as soon as we get to your place. You've got frozen peas, yes?"

"My place?"

"I'm not really in the mood to go out to dinner, so it's either your place or mine."

"Oh."

"Does that Thai place near you still deliver?"

"The Thai Bowl?"

"Yeah, that's the one."

"I think so, but I'm not eating that. If you want Thai I can make us some."

"But you won the bet. I have to supply dinner." Although the thought of Red cooking for him did give Zac a very pleasant swirl of warmth in the centre of his chest. He refused to look at the feeling too closely.

"I don't eat take-out, Zac. So it's either I cook for both of us or I cook for me and you order in."

"You don't eat take-out at all?" He knew she was strict about her diet. Had been since she'd overcome anorexia, but he hadn't had a clue she was this severe.

"Nope. I prefer to know what I'm putting in my body at all times."

"All times?"

"Am I cooking or not."

Zac shrugged. "I guess you're cooking." It didn't matter to him either way as long as he got to spend more time with her.

"Right. Okay then." Red turned back to the sink and finished washing the blender.

He wasn't sure where they were going but he figured dinner together was a start, plus, it would give him more time to work out what he was doing. With any luck—not that he'd had much of that today—she wouldn't be ordering him to go home afterwards.

FREDDIE KEPT SNEAKING glances at Zac. The minute they'd arrived at her place, she'd ordered him to sit and grabbed him a bag of frozen peas for his face. At some point in the last fifteen minutes, he'd fallen asleep on her couch and the bag had fallen to the floor. His nose was a little swollen and red but it didn't look too bad.

She'd wanted him to go home to get changed out of his bloody shirt but he'd resisted, and she'd finally relented by making him promise to wash it at her place. Of course that meant he was now bare-chested. All those sleek muscles on full display...

She shivered and her hands tingled with the memories of running her fingers over his sculptured pecs and abs. Playing with his flat nipples, making them hard...

"Hey." Zac stretched his arms over his head. "Dinner ready?"

"Ah, not yet." Freddie eyed the ingredients she'd yet to chop up. She'd been so busy staring at Zac's edible body that she hadn't done more than pull the veggies from the fridge. "It'll be about thirty minutes yet."

"Do you want some help?" he asked as he sat up and turned her way.

Jesus. She couldn't function with him halfway across the

room. If he actually came and stood beside her... "No. I've got it."

"Are you sure? I feel like a freeloader."

"You're injured."

"I'm not exactly crippled," he argued.

"No, but you should rest," she said and then murmured, "and it's my fault you're hurt."

"What?"

"Do you want the chili hot or mild?"

He cocked one eyebrow. "That's not what you said."

Freddie smiled. "Hot it is."

His eyes narrowed. "You're not responsible."

She sucked in a breath.

"Neither of us could have predicted two guys would use my face as a punching bag today."

Freddie sighed. "I might have had an idea West would. It's not the first time he's thrown a punch in my honour."

"Can't say I can blame him for that. He's your brother."

"So? I'm not fourteen and starving myself to death anymore." God dammit. She hated that it always seemed to come back to her illness.

Zac stood. "No. But it killed him. Hell, it killed all of us to see you like that."

"But I'm no longer that teenager."

He came towards her slowly, as though he didn't want to spook her, and she clenched her teeth to keep from yelling at him for treating her like fragile glass.

"You might not be that same girl, but none of us that saw you go through that can forget. We still see—"

Freddie held up her hand, palm out. "Don't. To quote you. No more talking. You're just going to piss me off."

"Red."

"Stop calling me that."

"Fine. Freddie."

She shook her head. "I mean it, Zac. Conversation over or I'm going to throw your arse out regardless of your bruised face."

He backed away a step. "Okay. No more talking."

"Good."

Turning back to the counter, Freddie took a deep breath and picked up the knife. She hated it when people looked at her like she was wounded. Like the slightest thing could set her off. Christ. It had been over ten years since she'd beaten the disease. Ten years of proving she was capable of functioning like anyone else.

God. She was a successful business owner. Had hundreds of patients who'd turned their lives around with her help. "How much more do I have to prove?"

"You don't need to prove anything."

"Shit." Freddie spun around, knife in hand and almost gutted Zac. "Don't do that!"

He grabbed her wrist with one hand and removed the knife from her grip with the other. Leaning over, he placed it on the counter and then took both her hands in his. "You are one of the strongest women I know. It doesn't mean I won't worry about you. Warranted or not, it's in our DNA to worry about the people we care about."

Her shoulders slumped, her rigid muscles relaxing. "I get that. I'm just tired of being looked at like I'll crack at the smallest thing. Shit. If that was going to happen, it would have been while I trudged my way through my double degree."

Zac laughed. "I hear ya there. Law school just about killed me."

Smiling she said, "Bullshit. You finished top of your class."

He frowned. "Who told you that?"

"West."

"How the hell does he know?"

"You didn't tell him?"

"Hell, no. I didn't even tell Coop."

"Oh." She shrugged. "I haven't a clue how he found out then."

Freddie thought the scowl on Zac's face was adorable, and the urge to kiss it away stole through her. She resisted. Barely. Pulling her hands from his, she turned back to the counter and the food she needed to chop. "I need to get dinner on."

She hoped Zac would take the hint and not push the subject any further. Being treated like a child always annoyed her. Made her want to behave like one and stomp her foot. Preferably on the foot of the person who was doing the annoying. Usually West.

Her brother could be such a shithead. She loved him, but his interference in her life—particularly her love life—had finally reached the limit of her patience. She'd put up with it until now because honestly, none of the guys he'd tried to intimidate were that important to her.

Zac was different. And she was only now beginning to understand how different.

ZAC LEFT Red alone and went back to the couch. They could both do with a little space. Something had shifted between them just now. He wasn't sure what or how, only that some indefinable thing had changed.

Easing back against the cushion, he watched her through lowered lashes. He didn't want her to think he was keeping an eye on her. He'd obviously hit a hot button. West was guilty of being overly protective where Red was concerned. Hell, Zac had been that way himself on more than one occasion. It was part of the reason he'd stayed away when he first realised his interest had turned to more than friendship.

He didn't have his head screwed on straight when it came to Red anymore. She'd been in the best friend's little sister category for so long that this new development in their relationship fucked with his mind and his heart. Zac didn't want to hurt her, but then he didn't want to leave her alone either.

Damned if he did. Damned if he didn't.

His phone vibrated in his pocket and he pulled it out to see a text from Coop. He hadn't replied to any of the messages or calls either his brother or best friend had sent him. Zac knew what they had to say and he didn't want to hear it. There was enough recrimination going on in his own head, he didn't need to hear it from either of them.

And besides. Red was right. She wasn't that broken teenage girl anymore. She'd more than proven she'd moved past the illness that had stolen two years of her life.

He'd be a fool not to see the remarkable woman she'd become. If she were anyone else...any other woman, he wouldn't be using such caution. Then again, it wasn't just her connection to his best friend to consider. There was the friendship he and Red had. It was solid and vital and Zac wasn't sure he was prepared to fuck with it.

Should have thought of that before you fucked her, *idiot.*

Bit late to develop a conscience, but there it was, messing with the already confused emotions surrounding Red. He couldn't decide if it was because of their pre-existing connection or if what he felt for her was different to any other woman he'd been with.

Whatever it was that was happening between them, he had to sort it out quickly.

For both their sakes.

6

ZAC COULD SMELL HER. Over the spicy scent of the meal Red had made was the tantalising fragrance of her skin—her arousal. It was subtle, but it was there, and it revved his own desire higher. Stirred and teased until he vibrated with need.

"Do you want more?" Red asked.

He wanted more. More of her. "No. I'm good."

"Are you sure? There's plenty left."

"Honestly, I'm full. It was surprisingly filling considering there's no meat in it."

Red laughed, the sound tripping over his skin and lighting fires in its wake. Without thought, Zac leaned over and pressed his mouth to hers. He kept it simple. Just lips on lips—no tongues. He wanted to savour. To fall slowly into the pleasure of kissing her.

But Red was having none of that. She thrust her tongue into his mouth and dared him to join in. Her boldness didn't end there. He praised their decision to eat on the couch when he found himself with a lapful of Red. She'd thrown one leg over his and pressed her chest to his. Zac wove his fingers into her hair and held her still so he could devour her mouth properly.

She whimpered when he sucked on her tongue. Rocked her hips against him and ground her pussy on his throbbing cock. Clothes separated them. Layers and layers of frustrating fabric they had to get rid of.

"Bedroom," he panted. "Don't want to do you here."

Red didn't protest when he stood with her in his arms. She wrapped her legs around his waist and her arms around his neck and let him carry her from the room. He knew his way around her house. He'd helped paint it when she'd first moved in. But he hadn't been in her bedroom. Not with furniture.

Certainly not with a king-size bed sitting front and centre.

Her room wasn't girly. The comforter was a deep blue, the bedhead, chest of drawers and bedsides were white. There were pictures on the walls of people and scenery, and Zac knew they were all photos Red had taken. He wanted to take the time to admire each one, but he couldn't resist the woman in his arms any longer.

He dropped her on the bed. "Strip," he ordered as he went to work on his jeans.

She scrambled backwards, kicking off her flip-flops and wiggling out of her shorts as she went. Her top came next. By the time Zac got his shoes off and pants down, she was spread out naked. He groaned. The woman was meant to be fucked. Putting one knee on the bed, he leaned over and wrapped his hand around her ankle.

"Don't move other than spreading those legs so I can get between them."

Zac crawled up, using his shoulders to open those sexy legs farther. He braced himself on his elbow, his face inches from her wet cunt. The musk of her arousal surrounded him, tempting him to taste. Flattening his tongue, he took what was on offer.

In one long sweep, he lapped at her. From bottom to top, he laved her once. "God, you taste amazing."

"Zac." She squirmed under him and he placed his palms on her thighs to hold her still.

"Can't get enough of you," he murmured against her slick folds before licking her up one side and down the other.

He couldn't get enough. Couldn't stop gorging on her tender flesh while she writhed and moaned. Zac had always liked going down on a woman. Liked their flavour and texture against his tongue—his lips. But Red was different. He loved eating her out. The sexy noises she made. The way her cunt clenched around the tip of his tongue when he shoved it inside her.

She was addictive.

His cock throbbed, but he ignored the ache. He wanted her to come on his face. Wanted to taste the richer flavour her orgasm produced.

Using his thumbs to part her folds, Zac put his mouth over her clit and sucked. She bucked beneath him and pain shot through his face when her pubic bone connected with his nose. He grunted but didn't stop. Couldn't stop. He needed that moment when she lost it. Needed it more than his own comfort or breath.

With his lips locked around that swollen bud of nerves, he worked his hand under his chin and drove two fingers into her quivering channel. Her cunt muscles gripped him. Slammed down around him with punishing force as the first spasm seized her. She clenched and unclenched. Each contraction sucked at his fingers while he sucked at her clit.

She thrashed and cried out. Zac soaked it all up until the last ripple of her climax ebbed away. He raised his head and looked up Red's trembling torso. Her breasts rose and fell with her ragged breath and a fine sheen of sweat coated her skin, giving her a silky shine. Zac couldn't resist the lure of all that flesh.

He moved up her body slowly. Licking and nipping, he took his time, making sure he didn't miss one sensitive inch of her with his mouth.

"Zac." Her voice was whispery soft. "Please."

Unable to deny her or himself anymore he quickened his pace until his mouth hovered over hers. "What? Tell me what you want."

"You." She slipped her hand around his waist and pulled his body down on hers. "I want you inside me."

Zac settle his hips between hers, nestled his cock in the slick heat of her cunt. "I want me inside you too." He drove his hips forward and thrust his entire length into her. "Forever. God. I want to stay buried inside you forever."

FOREVER.

The word echoed through her mind, but Freddie didn't have time to ponder what Zac meant. Or whether it was a heat-of-the-moment statement. He was already driving into her. Pushing her higher and higher with each body-slamming thrust of his cock. It wasn't enough.

She gripped his arse and tried to drag him closer. "Harder."

"God," he groaned into her ear. "You kill me."

"More." Freddie couldn't explain the sudden need—the desperation—slicing into her. "C'mon, Zac, fuck me like you mean it."

"I am fucking you," he panted against her neck.

"You call this fucking me?" She chuckled.

Freddie wasn't sure why she was pushing him. Why she

needed more. Whatever *more* was. But she wanted him to lose control. Wanted to break him. Needed to connect in a way no other woman had and she knew she could. If he'd just let her.

"Red." He nipped her cheek. "Don't push me."

Laughter burst from her throat. "You don't think I can take you? Think I can't handle what you've got, Zac?"

"Red," he growled right before he bit her chin.

"C'mon, Zac." God, what was she doing? He was taking her hard enough to bruise now, and still it wasn't enough. "Gimme more."

"Damn you." Zac gripped her face in his hands. "No more talking."

Freddie gasped when he pulled out of her. Before she could get her breath back he dragged her off the bed and spun her around. He pushed her to her knees and bent her over.

"Lie on the bed." He pressed his hand between her shoulder blades and moved in behind her. "You want me to give it to you, Red?"

God. The gravel in his voice vibrated over her skin. She whimpered. Actually whimpered.

"Think you can take me, do ya?" He grabbed a handful of her hair and pulled her head back. His lips brushed her ear. "You know what I want, right? I want your arse, Red. Are you gonna give it to me?"

Oh God. "Y-yes," she hissed between her teeth as his cock probed at her back entrance.

He laughed. The rumble of his chest shuddered along her spine. "Not tonight. In spite of the fact you want it, you're not ready and I won't hurt you, Red."

"But—"

Zac angle his hips and drove his cock into her pussy. "Shh..." He licked along her neck, nipped at her jaw. "I'm gonna give it to you now."

He gave a slight tug on her hair before letting her go. His big hands gripped her hips and Freddie curled her fingers into the bedding as he slowly dragged his cock out of her clenching pussy. She thought he was going to torture her with gentle slow thrusts, but the second only his cockhead remained inside her, he slammed back in again.

He took her hard.

He took her fast.

And all she could do was hold on. He gripped her hips, his thumbs pulling her cheeks apart as he continued to drive into her.

"God. I'll never get enough of watching you take my cock."

"Zac." She pushed back as he plunged forward. "Please. I need…"

"Yeah, I know." He leaned over her again, his chest pressing her deeper into the bed. "I've got you."

Working one hand under her, Zac slipped his fingers between her legs and found her clit. He circled and pressed. Thrust. Circled and pressed. Thrust.

"Please," she cried. Freddie couldn't take much more. She was twisted and tight and burning up from the inside out. "Zac. Please."

He skimmed his teeth over her shoulder. "Almost. There."

Picking up the pace with his maddening fingers, he took her up. His hips pounded faster.

"Almost," he panted. "C'mon, Red. Come with me."

He pinched her clit and sank his teeth into the corded muscle of her neck as he powered deeper.

She shattered.

With a muffled cry, she buried her face into the bed and exploded.

Zac growled in her ear as he followed her. His cock throbbed inside her as he emptied spurt after spurt of come. It seemed as though he came forever, each pulse sending ripples of pleasure cascading through her.

Her hands and feet tingled. Breath sawed in and out of lungs too weak to keep up with the rush of blood in her veins. And her heart... It beat against her sternum like a battering ram. At any moment, she expected to crack a rib.

"Fuck."

"Mmm..." Freddie couldn't manage a word.

"Maybe we should keep talking."

"Huh?"

"Every time we shut up you kill me." He pulled from her body with a groan before falling to the bed beside her.

"You've got it wrong." She turned to face him and opened her eyes. "You're the one doing the killing."

Zac grinned and rolled to his side. He brushed the hair from her face. "I think the killing is mutual."

"Maybe." Freddie knew he killed her body and heart. She wasn't so sure she did the same to him.

"C'mon. Let's shower."

"Jesus. What is it with you and showering after sex?"

He waggled his eyebrows. "I like you all wet and slippery."

Freddie groaned.

Zac laughed. "C'mon." He grabbed her arm as he sat up. "I'll carry you."

Without effort, he scooped her up and carried her across the room to her en suite. For a lawyer who spent all his time in an office or the courtroom, he certainly had muscles.

She'd let him carry her anywhere, because once this thing blew up in their faces—and it was bound to, they flashed too hot and too fast for this to last—he'd probably never talk to her again, never mind touch her.

. . .

ZAC HELD A SLEEPY, damp woman in his arms and he never wanted to let her go. He'd never felt this way. With every other woman who'd passed through his life—his bed—he couldn't have cared less if they stayed or went. This one...

Red.

Jesus. He wanted so much from her. He wanted so many things he couldn't get them straight in his head. She turned him inside out and upside down without effort, and she didn't even have a clue.

He'd expected them to go at it again in the shower, only once he had her in there, all he'd wanted to do was to take care of her. They'd washed each other. The gentle strokes of soaped hands a sensual caress that neither had felt the need to take farther. And now, they were cuddled together in her bed.

And it was enough.

He couldn't recall ever lying in bed with a woman and not wanting or having sex. Sure they'd already gone at it a time or two or fifty in the last twenty-four hours, but he wasn't sated. Not by a long shot. Except what he wanted didn't fall into the fuck category.

For the first time in Zac's life, he wanted to love a woman. Wanted to make love to her in slow, soul-touching ways so she'd never leave him.

Fuck.

He was in love with Red.

In love with his best friend's little sister.

She stirred beside him as his grip tightened around her.

How the hell was he going to deal with this?

Lust he knew. He could handle wanting to fuck her. Hell, he had handled it.

But loving her?

How the hell was he supposed to do that?

"What's the matter? Is your nose hurting?" Red murmured.

"Huh?" Zac latched on to the excuse for his sudden tension. "Yeah. A little."

"I'll get you some more pain meds." She slipped out of his arms and off the bed.

Without a stich of clothing, she left the room. Left him alone with his jumbled thoughts and the rush of panic flooding his veins. He was going to screw this up. He'd already screwed it up.

His best friend was going to kill him.

He'd betrayed West over and over again from the minute he'd thought about getting Red naked. And now he'd gone and done the unimaginable. He'd fallen for the one woman he shouldn't have.

He had to go.

Had to get out of here and think. He couldn't do that with Red in his arms. Throwing back the cover, he'd swung his feet over the side of the bed when she came into the room.

"What are you doing?" She walked towards him. A naked temptation no man should be forced to resist.

"I should head home."

"Oh." Her mouth turned down at the ends.

"We've both got work tomorrow."

"Okay." Red chewed her lip and Zac wanted to kiss her to make her stop.

"I've got an early meeting." He didn't.

"Right." She put two pills and a glass of water on the bedside table next to him. "Take the meds before you go."

"Thanks."

She shrugged and turned away. "No problem."

Zac wanted to kick his own arse. He was being a dick, but he couldn't stay with her another second. Not when he knew he couldn't give her more than he already had. There were so many reasons why being with her at all was wrong. He'd been a selfish prick to touch her at all.

"I really do have an early meeting," he lied. He'd say anything to take that look off her face.

"Sure." She smiled, but it didn't reach her eyes, and his gut twisted tighter.

"Red—"

"It's fine, Zac. I've got a full day tomorrow too. Make sure you lock the door on your way out." She slid beneath the covers on the opposite side of the bed and faced the far wall.

He blew out a breath. Standing, he looked around for his jeans. Scooping them up off the floor, he looked at Red one last time. She'd dismissed him, and it was nothing less than he deserved, but he didn't know how to fix this. Didn't know how to give her what she wanted from him. How to get what he wanted.

Or even if it was possible.

7

ZAC OPENED the front door and wished he hadn't.

West charged past him. Coop stood with his hands shoved into his front pockets on the porch.

"Mind if we come in?" Coop asked with a half grin.

Zac moved aside. "No. By all means, come in."

"At least he didn't punch you," Coop said.

"There is that." Considering Zac's nose still hurt a week after Red's muscle-bound crusader had thumped him, it was a good thing West hadn't taken another swing at him.

He followed Coop into the living room where West paced. He'd known to expect his friend, but he'd figured the guy would at least go home from the airport before arriving on his doorstep.

"How was the honeymoon?" Zac asked.

West grunted.

Okay. No chit-chat. "Say what you have to. But if you take a swing, it won't be a free shot like last time." Zac crossed his arms and braced his feet shoulder width apart.

"Relax, Zac. West isn't going to hit you," his brother said

and chuckled. "Not if he wants to have sex with his wife ever again."

Zac raised an eyebrow.

West stopped pacing and turned to stare out the window. "Meddling woman," he grumbled.

Quiet settled around them, and Zac gave it a minute before his patience got the better of him. "As much fun as this silent treatment is, you could have done it from your house."

West shot him a glare.

Coop laughed.

Zac failed to see what his brother found so funny in this shitty situation. He sighed. "Look—"

"No." West turned to face him. "Do you love her?"

What the fuck?

"I know you wouldn't mess with her if she was just a quick fuck, Zac." West dragged a hand down his face. "I know you. You've never used a woman like that and you certainly wouldn't do that with Freddie. At least the guy I know wouldn't, and your brother assures me you haven't changed your morals to those of an alley cat."

Zac glanced at Coop. "I don't use women, no." He turned back to West. "Why are you here exactly?"

West sucked in a deep breath and let it out. "We were talking." He indicated Coop.

"When? You've been on your honeymoon."

"Let's just say I spent a lot of my week away on the phone," West said. "Not all of it pleasantly."

"Huh?"

"Not only was I copping a mouthful from my lovely wife, who by the way held out because of what happened last week. But I also copped it from my sister." West rubbed his fingers back and forth on his forehead. "It seems I've been a little overzealous in my big-brother role, and according to her, I owe you an apology."

"Wow. Red told you to apologise?" So she didn't hate him then. Zac had thought she'd be sending her brother around to finish off what he'd started last week, not to say sorry.

"Red?" West's brow wrinkled.

"Freddie," Zac clarified.

West's eyebrows shot up into his hair. "Oh my God." He laughed.

Zac didn't get what was funny and a look at Coop didn't enlighten him. "Why are you laughing?"

"You call her Red."

"Ah, yeah..."

West laughed harder. "To remind yourself to stay away."

Zac jolted. "How the hell do you know that? Did she tell you?"

West shook his head. "No." He finally got his humour under control and took a deep breath. "It's so you."

Okay, so West knew him.

"Which means Kelsey is right."

"What?" Zac was lost. "What has Kelsey got to do with it?"

"You're in love with my sister."

Oh shit. "Ah..." He wasn't going to deny or confirm. If he was going to acknowledge the emotion he held for Red out loud, it wouldn't be to her brother before her.

"You're a dick, you know that?" West asked.

Zac didn't take offense. He figured at this point he *was* a dick. He was certainly fucked like one.

"I'm only going to say this once and then you're on your own." West walked over to him and clamped a hand on Zac's shoulder. "Don't let her get away. Don't let who her brother is cost you the woman you love."

Zac opened his mouth but nothing came out.

"I know what I'm talking about. Don't let other people get in the way, Zac." West squeezed his shoulder before moving past him.

Coop slapped him on the back. "You should think about who that advice just came from. If anyone knows about letting something go for all the wrong reasons, it's West."

Zac stood frozen in place until the front door banged shut. Jerked out of his thoughts, he spun around to find West and Coop gone.

He'd known before they arrived that he wasn't going to walk away from Red. He just hadn't figured out how he was going to approach her.

Okay, he hadn't worked out the best way to grovel.

He also hadn't had a clue how to tell West that he was chucking out the friend-code book and going after his little sister. Now he didn't have to worry about that part of his dilemma.

The one thing Zac did know was that even if it took every day for the rest of his life, he was going to convince Frederica Mann that she was meant to be his.

FREDDIE GOT off the couch with a sigh and the echo of her doorbell. She'd expected to see West sometime today. His plane had landed a few hours ago, and if she were honest, she was a little surprised he hadn't shown up before now.

She unlocked the door without looking through the peephole. Pulling it open as she turned away, she said, "How was your week?"

"It sucked."

Freddie froze.

Zac.

She closed her eyes and hoped she could get through the

next few minutes without dropping to her knees and begging. Forcing her mouth into a smile, Freddie turned and faced the man who'd walked out with her heart last weekend.

"Hello, Zac."

"Can I come in?"

Sucking in a deep breath, she nodded. "Suit yourself." Did her voice wobble a bit? Did it sound like she didn't care either way?

"Can we talk?" he asked as he stepped inside and closed the door.

Freddie laughed. "Talk? I seem to recall you telling me not to on a number of occasions."

He flinched.

Good. At least he felt something.

"I'll never tell you to stop talking again."

She raised one eyebrow. "I doubt we'll find ourselves in a position for you to want me to shut up ever again." Her heart ached. She wanted more than anything for him to tell her to stop talking. Freddie still didn't have a clue what had happened to make him leave and not call—not come round. She'd never understand his hot-and-cold behaviour.

"I deserve that."

Freddie smiled. He deserved that and more. She just wasn't sure why he did or why she should give him the cold shoulder.

Everything inside her wanted to wrap her arms around him and hold him tight.

No doubt about it. The man had a hold on her but good.

"Do you want a drink?" she asked as she turned and led the way to the kitchen.

"No, thanks."

So polite. She perched her hip against the counter and waited.

Zac stopped a few feet away. He shoved his hands in his

back pockets. Pulled them out. Pushed them into his front pockets. Pulled them out again.

Nice to know he was nervous. He probably thought her brother would be hunting him down. She decided to set his mind at ease on that score.

"West isn't going to come after you. I've spoken to him and reminded him that who I sleep with isn't his business."

"I know."

"You know?"

He ran his hands through his hair. "He came to see me."

Freddie didn't think she'd ever seen Zac so frazzled. Even when she'd pushed him until he'd lost control, he hadn't had this...tattered, unraveled look. "When?"

"About an hour ago."

"Oh."

"It's not what you think."

Freddie laughed. "Zac, with you I never know what to think."

"I'm sorry."

"For what?"

"Everything."

Air hissed through her teeth as she sucked in a breath. "Everything?"

"No." He took a step forward. "Not that. Never that."

He ran his fingers through his hair again. "God. Sleeping with you was the only good thing I did." He rocked back on his heels. "I'll never be sorry for touching you. I'm sorry for all the rest."

"I'm not following, Zac." If he didn't regret having sex with her then why had he left?

"I screwed up. I'm still screwing up." He paced to the side. "I can't seem to think when I'm around you. No. That's a lie. I think. I think about getting your clothes off and getting inside you so I can breathe. I can't seem to breathe when I'm not with you. Why is that?" He stopped and stared at her.

"Ah..."

"I'll tell you why." He moved towards her. "Because I love you."

"I...um...of course you do. We've known each other forever. You love me like you love Cassie."

"No. Not like Cassie at all." He moved in front of her, put his hands on her hips and pulled her to her to toes. "I'm *in* love with you, Freddie."

She sucked in a breath. "You used my name."

Zac laughed. "Out of everything I just said, *that* was the one thing you heard?"

"You haven't said my name in months." Oh my God. The man had just professed his love for her and all she could focus on was that he'd finally called her by her name.

"I don't want to warn myself away anymore. The only red I want to think about is the colour of your body when I make you come."

"But what about West?"

"West who?"

She smiled. "My brother."

"You have a brother?" He arched one eyebrow. "You should introduce us some time."

Freddie laughed. "You're a dickhead."

"No. I *was* acting like a dickhead. I'm not now. The only dick around here is in my pants and really wants to be in yours."

"Oh my God. That's so cheesy."

"But you like cheesy, right?" He leaned forward and brushed his mouth on hers. "You secretly love it. Right?"

She wasn't sure she should give in to this man so easily. He could crush her with the flick of an eyelash.

"I promise I won't play fast and loose with your heart, Freddie. If you trust me with it, I'll cherish it until my dying breath."

"Zac."

"I promise. And if I ever treat it, or you, badly again, you can get your brother and that muscle-bound Pierce to beat me black and blue."

"Zac."

"What?"

"No more talking."

"NO MORE TALKING?" She had to listen to him. He had to convince her to forgive him.

Freddie shook her head. "No more talking."

"But—"

"Zac." She grinned at him.

"So if we're not talking then we're—"

"You're still talking, Zac."

"I know but..." Was she telling him what he thought? She hadn't kicked him out but then she hadn't reciprocated his declaration of love either.

"Zac!"

"What?" He couldn't think. She was in his arms. He'd told her he loved her.

"For God's sake." She slipped out of his hold and grabbed his hand. "C'mon."

"What? Where?"

"You know, as much as I like the fact I seem to be able to ruffle the unruffleable Zachary Moreland, I kinda like it when he's in control."

"You want me to be in control?" Zac shook his head to clear some of the cobwebs of confusion tangling his brainwaves.

She led him into her bedroom and suddenly his mind was crystal clear.

"No more talking," he murmured.

"What?" Freddie stopped beside the bed.

He moved in on her. "No more talking, Freddie. I can't think straight when you're talking, and I've got other, better, ideas that you can use your mouth for."

"Yeah?" She grinned as she climbed onto the bed backwards. "Are they dirty things?"

Zac closed his eyes for a second. "Fuck. You're going to be the death of me woman."

"But what a way to go. My mouth wrapped around—"

"No more talking." He crowded her until she lay down. "No. More. Talking."

"I love you too."

"Ah, fuck." Zac laid his forehead on hers. "*Now* you say it."

She giggled. "I can take it back."

"Don't you dare." He grabbed her hands and dragged them up beside her head to pin them in place. "Say it again."

"I love you."

He kissed her. "Again."

"I love you, Zac."

This time the kiss wasn't quick, but he cut it off before he sank too deep into the pleasure to pull back. "Once more."

"I love you."

"Okay." He sat up and grabbed the hem of her shirt. With her help, he got it over her head and then did the same with his. "Now."

She blinked up at him.

"No. More. Talking."

DARE YOU TO

To all those who dare to follow their hearts.
And to Mr.C for taking on the biggest dare of all. Me.

1

"DARE YOU TO."

A breath shuddered through Shaye's lips and her eyelids lowered as those three words whispered in her ear. She knew if she turned a fraction to the side, the person who'd spoken them would be close.

So close she could count the gold flecks in his hazel eyes.

So close their breaths would mingle.

So close she could steal the kiss she wanted desperately.

She shivered.

They hadn't kissed. Not in all the months they'd flirted. They'd come close—oh so close—but Shaye hadn't been able to take that final step.

Until now.

She knew he was taunting her with his words, but she'd be lying if she said she wasn't ready. She'd also be lying if she didn't admit she was ready because she knew there was no way she could lose her heart. Not now she was moving thousands of miles away. It was safe to tangle with him when she wouldn't have to watch him move on to the next woman when he was done with her.

And he would be done.

Shaye had watched it time and time again over the last eight years. Not that he was a man-whore or anything. The opposite really. He was selective and he stuck. For months. But never longer.

"Shaye?"

Jesus. His voice alone did her in. That husky sound vibrated over her nerves like the sweeping caress of a lover's hand on her skin. She'd heard it long before she'd set eyes on him. Sight unseen, she'd fallen in lust. Completely. Days after hearing that molten-sex voice on her best friend's voicemail, Shaye had gotten her first glimpse of its owner.

Cooper Moreland.

The guy totally lived up to the sexy rasp.

Broad shoulders, mouthwatering chest and washboard abs, and his arms... Thick with muscles earned from hard work, they drew her in a way she'd never experienced. Hell, everything about Cooper Moreland drew her like no other guy ever had.

Coop—to his friends, and by default her—had starred in every one of her secret fantasies since the day the husky timber of his voice had stroked over her senses.

God. She'd spent years getting off to the image of him. She even had to own up to occasionally squeezing her eyes closed and pretending whatever guy she was with was Coop.

No more pretending though.

She'd made up her mind to go for it. For the next month, she was going to get her fill of Cooper Moreland and leave her adopted home of Sydney to return to her native Perth a well-satisfied woman. Ready to take on a new job—a dream job—and the rest of her life without the gnawing ache she'd lived with since she'd met him.

"Shaye?" Warm air fanned over the side of her face, and she could swear his lips brushed her cheek.

She turned her head, caught his gaze with hers and held it. It was now or never. Without a word, she moved away from his heat and slid out of the booth. Come hell or high water, she was taking Coop's dare and upping the ante.

He didn't know it yet, but for the next thirty days, she was turning up the heat and burning this searing attraction out of her system.

COOP SUCKED IN A BREATH.

Fuck.

Was she really going to do it? He watched Shaye's sexy arse as she walked away. Kept his eyes glued to that mouthwatering, world-class rear end until it disappeared into the crowded bar.

Fuck.

He never thought she'd take him up on his dare. Shit, they'd been throwing out one-liners, come-ons and sexual innuendos for months, but not once had either of them taken the bait.

Not that he was sure she was doing that now. Maybe she was playing with him again. God knows, she'd done it before. He'd spent months with a perpetual hard-on. One he'd jacked off countless times while imagining Shaye in every dirty way his filthy mind could think up. And there'd been many. Some had even surprised him.

He'd always had a healthy sex drive and he hadn't shied away from trying things that came to mind or were suggested by the woman he was with, but he'd never—*never*—wanted to the carnal depths Shaye inspired. He wasn't even sure he had the balls to do half of what he'd fantasized about.

A shudder raked his spine and heat throbbed in his groin. Fuck. He'd have another full-blown hard-on by the time she came back just from the wondering—the anticipation.

"So Zac and Freddie. Never would have picked that," Toby said.

Coop glanced in his brother's direction. "They're a good fit."

"Didn't say they weren't. Just that I'd never have picked it."

"Explains why he's been a monumental arsehole these last few months," West said. "Poor bastard hasn't just had love screwing with his head. He's been dealing with guilt."

"Not to mention fear," Kelsey added.

"Of what?" West asked.

"Of you knocking his head off. Which, I'll point out, you almost did." Kelsey smiled at her husband.

West shrugged and reached for his beer. "Hey. Any big brother would do the same for their little sister."

"I don't recall any of the Moreland boys doing that when Luc hooked up with Cassie," Kelsey said before taking a sip of her wine, her smile hidden behind the glass.

Coop grimaced. It wasn't like he or one of his brothers hadn't decked one of Cassie's boyfriend's in the past.

"Christ. Are you insane woman? Have you seen Luc?" Toby asked. "Fuck. You'd need an army to take him on. Or a death wish."

"Plus, you'd need to *know* something was going on." Coop picked at the label on his beer. "And as usual, we're the last to know what goes on in our little sister's life."

"Smart woman," Kelsey murmured.

Coop laughed. "Yes. Cassie is definitely switched on when it comes to hiding things from us."

"After the way you lot hovered over her in high school, I'm surprise she didn't take out restraining orders," Kelsey added.

Toby caught Coop's eye and they burst out laughing.

"I fail to see what's funny about that," Kelsey said.

"It's funny because she threatened each of them with one on a number of occasions," West said. "But then she got smart."

Both Coop and Toby groaned.

Kelsey sat forward. "Oh, do tell. *This* sounds like it might be funny."

West chuckled. "Let's just say getting a taste of their own medicine was a real eye opener, and the Moreland boys all took a cautious step back when it came to their little sister's love life."

"Shame you didn't learn from their mistakes." Kelsey smiled.

"Hey!" West protested.

Coop clapped his best friend on the back. "You got one good punch in, that's what counts." He grinned. But the curve of his lips froze—along with every muscle in his body—when he spotted Shaye heading back to their table.

He watched the sway of her hips, the bounce of her breasts and the smooth mile of tan legs visible beneath her short skirt. His stupid gaze ricocheted between those three enticing spots on her body until it settled on her hips. Narrowing his eyes, he tried to determine if she'd gone through with the dare, but the slinky top she wore flirted with the area he most wanted to see.

"Speaking of hooking up," Toby murmured. "You gone there yet, Coop?"

"Shut up," he growled.

"Nope. Not yet." West laughed. "No man getting any is as wound up as Coop is."

"Which bit of shut up did you not understand?"

"Who's shutting up?" Shaye slid into the booth beside him. "Who's saying what now? What'd I miss?"

"Nothing," Coop said.

Shaye's gaze swung to Kelsey, but her best friend wasn't giving anything away. And for once, much to Coop's relief, his brother and his best friend had listened, and both remained mute. All three of them picked up their drinks and glanced around the bar. Shaye frowned, but thankfully she let it go without further comment.

Coop was dying to know if Shaye had taken the dare, but there was no way to tell without asking or groping her in public. And wouldn't that get their relationship, or whatever the hell this was, some more unwanted attention from their friends.

Even knowing the futility of the action, he couldn't stop himself from continuously slanting his gaze to her side trying to discern the answer he craved. She dropped her bag on the seat between them, making the slim chance of finding out what he wanted to know a zero possibility.

"Oh, hey, I found those mints you wanted." Shaye's voice was low, no more than a whisper, and he doubted anyone else heard her over the music pumping through the bar's sound system.

Before Coop could work out what the fuck she was talking about, Shaye opened her bag, and right there on top was the reddest, flimsiest thong he'd ever seen. Blood rushed through his veins straight to his groin where his cock instantly thickened. His heart thumped against his ribcage so hard all the air was pushed from his lungs.

"Fuck." Coop wasn't sure if the husky word was a prayer for help or of gratitude.

He didn't know why he did it or even when he'd thought about doing it, but he had that scrap of lace fisted in his hand and was shoving it in his pocket before he pulled in a breath.

"Hey!"

Coop moved his gaze to Shaye's. Emotions he couldn't decipher flitted through her eyes before she registered the look on his face—in his eyes—and she sucked a breath through her teeth, her bottom lip trembling.

"Mine." The growl rumbled in his throat, but the sound came from deep in his gut where his insides were blazing with the need to get her under him. Over him. Against him. Surrounding him.

Hell, any and every way he could get her as long as they were naked.

Now.

COOP GRABBED Shaye's arm and nudged her along the seat with his hard thigh against hers. "Let's go."

She barely had time to grab her bag before he squashed it between them. "What?"

"We'll be late for our reservation," he said as he maneuvered them out of the booth.

"What reservation?" She tried to stop her forward momentum, but Coop had her on her feet and turned in the direction of the exit before she could blink.

"Catch you all later," he threw over his shoulder.

"Coop, what the hell are you doing?" she asked as he tugged her with him.

He leaned close and whispered in her ear. "Say goodbye, Shaye."

She could see he was speaking through clenched teeth and the look in his eyes revealed he was a man on the edge.

Holy shit.

She'd never inspired that look in anyone before. Lifting her hand, she gave an absentminded wave and a murmured goodbye that no one but Coop would hear. But she couldn't take her eyes off his. Couldn't think beyond the heat and desire flooding her body. She just managed to walk without falling on her arse as he all but dragged her out of the bar and across the parking lot to his truck.

When they reached the passenger door, she found hard metal pressed against her back and Coop's hot body pressed against her front.

His face loomed over hers. "You took the dare."

"I..." She licked her lips, her mouth dry, her throat constricted. "Um..."

"Are we done dancing around this?"

"Dancing? This?" God. Why couldn't she think straight? The only thing running through her mind was the delicious press of all that hot, hard muscle and how she wished they were naked. Wished for his mouth to be on hers.

He smiled. "Yeah. We're done." His gaze lowered to her mouth and Shaye's insides tightened. "No more mucking around."

Shaye couldn't answer. Not with the heat of his gaze on her lips and his rough-skinned hand sliding up the outside of her thigh, around the back and pushing beneath her skirt to palm her bare arse. Her breath shuddered in her chest when he squeezed her exposed flesh.

"Now we're fucking around." His words sucked every last atom of oxygen from her body.

Before she could react, he slanted his mouth over hers.

His kiss was as carnal as she'd imagined it would be. He thrust his tongue between her lips, the move brutal and demanding, but at the same time seductive—electrifying. The sensations the rough caress delivered made her want to let him take whatever he wanted. Made Shaye want to follow Coop into the dark pleasure his mouth on hers promised.

She moaned when he nipped her bottom lip, tugged it down and out as he pulled her into him, both his hands now palming her arse. The hard ridge of his cock ground against her clit and her pussy clenched, her hips bucking forward to hold on to the hot pressure.

Coop moved his lips lightly over hers as he lifted her up. "Wrap your legs around me."

His voice rumbled thick and heavy in his chest, his breath ragged with each word, and Shaye shivered with the wave of lush desire that saturated her system at the sound. She didn't think to protest Coop's demand or about anything other than getting closer to the heat and hardness he continued to grind against her aching clit.

"Tighter," he growled. "Cross your ankles and hold on."

Shaye gripped his shoulders, digging in her short nails as he walked to the back of his truck. "What are you doing?"

"Moving out of sight."

"Oh, um..." Shaye knew she should stop him. If she didn't, there was no doubt in her mind that she'd let him fuck her in the car park up against his car. But for the life of her, she couldn't do it. Not yet. Not when each step the roll of his cock over her clit left her without the brainpower to speak. She'd stop him soon.

Just a few more seconds of pleasure...

2

COOPER PRESSED Shaye against his truck and used his body to pin her there while he adjusted his hold on her arse. Having those plush globes cupped in his hands had to rank in the top five highlights of his life. The feel of her silky skin was better than he'd imagined.

He slipped his hands lower. His fingertips encountered heat a split second before they hit the slick, moist folds of her cunt. "Fuck. You're soaking." Unable to resist, he shoved his fingers deeper.

She gasped and rocked against him. "Cooper."

His name fell from her mouth in a needy little rasp that sent a bolt of lust straight through his balls. He couldn't wait to get inside her. But first he wanted to make her come. He wanted to watch her fly apart in his arms before he buried himself inside her and made her do it again. "Right here."

"We have to sto—"

He circled her swollen clit.

"Oh God…"

Coop loved the way her words trailed off on a moan and

wanted to see if he could get her to make that sexy little sound again. Her breath caught in her throat as he dragged his fingers from her clit, through her hot, wet folds and all the way up into the crease of her arse. And when he toyed with the ring of puckered flesh hidden there, Shaye bucked against him, her legs gripping his waist tighter, her hips rolling with the stroke of his fingers.

She obviously wasn't opposed to a little anal play. He shuddered with the dark thrill of seeing just how far she'd go with him, but before he could push any further—test her boundaries—laughter burst through the hot summer night and grounded him to the here and now. They'd have to save the good stuff for somewhere private, but he wasn't letting her go without giving her a taste of what he could deliver.

"S-stop." She panted against his neck as he swiped his fingers through the wet crease of her cunt to her clit once more. "God. I'm going to come."

He chuckled. "That's the idea."

"No." She tensed in his arms. "Not here."

"Yes. Here. Now." Not giving her a chance to argue Coop dipped his head and took her mouth with his.

She was so hot and wet. Her mouth. Her cunt. Both offered him a world of bliss, and he was taking this small sample because he just couldn't help himself now that he had his hands and mouth on her.

He kissed her hard. He kissed her soft. And the whole time he worked his mouth over hers, his fingers plied her clit and teased her cunt. She took one finger, then two. Sexy little noises gurgled in her throat and her hips rocked as she moved with him.

Coop loved the taste of her on his tongue—the feel of her on his hands. She was his ultimate fantasy. Hot. Plush. Pliant. Everywhere he touched her, she yielded. It blew his mind and almost blew his cock. If she didn't fall over the edge soon, he'd be going with her. As it was, he could feel a wet patch of pre-come on his boxers.

Easing back from her mouth, he whispered against her lips. "Let go, Shaye. You know you want to."

"Can't. God." Her breath hitched. "Shouldn't feel. This good."

He licked back into her mouth and tangled his tongue with hers while increasing the pressure and speed of his fingers between her legs. Driving deep, Coop curled his fingers and searched for that elusive spot inside her. He knew the second he found it.

She jolted as though he'd zapped her with a volt of electricity. Her cunt clamped around his fingers and held him tight for a split second before she burst into motion. Coop had to press her harder against his truck to keep her writhing body within his grasp. He couldn't remember a woman ever falling apart in his arms so completely.

Her hips rocked on his hands, her tongue spearing into his mouth as if she wanted to crawl inside him. And the fingers she'd tangled in his hair fisted, the resulting yank on his scalp slamming through him like a punch to the gut. A growl tore up his throat and he bucked his hips in time with hers, coming closer than he ever had to spilling in his pants like a horny teenager getting his first touch of cunt.

Coop swallowed her cries of release and tried to keep from coming as he rode the wave of her climax. As the last ripples rolled through her body and into his, Shaye slumped against him. Their mouths separated and he held her close, tucking her face into his neck while they tried to regain reality —sanity.

At least that's what he was doing.

Gut instinct had told him they'd be explosive, but that

seemed too tame a word for what had just happened. And he hadn't even fucked her yet.

He slipped his hands from between her legs, the walls of her cunt sucking at his fingers and drawing a moan from both of them. Cupping her arse in one hand, he smoothed the other up her back and curled it around her neck.

He still hadn't caught his breath, but Shaye was trembling and breathing hard like she'd run a marathon and was on the verge of collapsing. "You okay?"

OKAY?

Shit. Shaye wasn't sure she was still alive. She'd just experienced the most explosive orgasm of her life. Her whole body was numb. The tingling, good kind of numb. And only one thought swirled in her head.

More.

She was pretty sure she'd never be okay again. The other thing she was sure of was that she was in trouble.

Big trouble.

If Coop could do that with only his hands, while fully clothed, in a goddamn fucking parking lot, she'd never survive the next month with her heart intact. Not when that traitorous organ had been hooked on him before he'd ever touched her. And it could only get better—or worse depending how you looked at it—with their clothes off, without the chance of getting caught, with time to explore...

She'd made a tactical error. A huge one. She'd underestimated their chemistry, her attraction, his skill. The unrelenting burn that filled her veins, scorched her bones and drove her to such desperation for his touch that she'd let him have her against his truck in a public parking lot.

"Shaye?" Coop's lips brushed her temple. "You okay?"

Unable to put words together yet, she nodded.

His arms tightened around her. "Let's get you in the truck."

She didn't protest when he moved them back to the passenger door and opened it without letting her go. He placed her on the seat but didn't step away. Instead, he tipped her head back with two fingers beneath her chin so he could meet her gaze.

"You sure you're okay?"

Shaye could see his concern. Wished she could get herself together enough to be her usual carefree self, but he'd shattered her with that orgasm, and she was still trying to pull the pieces back together.

Coop trailed his fingers along her jaw, beneath her ear and down the slope of her neck to her shoulder. "It's not often Shaye Adams is speechless."

His grin was a little smug, his eyes sparkling with masculine power, and Shaye suddenly had the perfect reason to find some of her usual bravado and her voice. "Well, I'm just trying to find the right words to say. I'd hate to crush your delicate male ego by using the wrong ones."

Coop's eyes narrowed. "The right words?"

"Hmm..." Shaye wiggled back in the seat to put some space between them.

Big mistake.

He leaned in as he shoved his hand up her skirt and cupped her pussy. "No chance of crushing my ego, Shaye. The evidence is coating your cunt and thighs. Not to mention my hands."

She gasped when he drove two fingers inside her, pumped them twice then pulled them free and bought his hand up between their faces. There was no way to evade him when he gripped the back of her neck with his free hand and used those wet fingers to paint her lips.

"Lick them," he growled.

Her lips parted on a rush of air and Cooper took advantage, pushing his fingers into her mouth. The taste and scent was unmistakably hers. She knew what he was trying to do, except now the fog from her orgasm had begun to clear and she wasn't about to let him keep her off balance a moment longer. She'd put him on equally shaky ground.

Shaye curled her tongue around his fingers as she closed her lips and sucked them deep. His eyelids lowered, thick, dark lashes shielding his gaze as he watched her take what he offered. She sucked harder. Used her teeth to scrape over his rough skin. Then she turned it up. With a small moan, she closed her eyes and treated his fingers like she would his cock.

In and out.

Suck and release.

Teeth and tongue.

The rumble of sound he made in his throat was unlike anything she'd ever heard before. It vibrated over her skin, down her spin and through her core, tightening and heating tissue still swollen and sensitive.

"Fuck." Coop yanked his hand away, but before she could protest the sudden change, he replaced his fingers with his tongue.

He ate at her mouth. Teeth, tongues and lips smashed together. Sucking, licking, biting. It was out of control and desperate. She'd never been kissed with such hunger. Such savage urgency.

Gasping for breath, Shaye tore her mouth from his. But Coop didn't let that stop him. He nipped at her chin. Licked under her jaw. Sucked on her neck.

"Need to taste you."

The words had barely left Coop's mouth when he dropped

to his knees, shoved her legs wider and buried his face in her pussy.

"Oh God." Her head dropped back, her hands going to his shoulders, her fingers grappling for purchase in a world that shook her from the inside out.

He growled against her, the sound beating against her clit and sending pulses of pleasure through her core. With the same desperate, out-of-control savagery he'd used on her mouth, Cooper drove her to the peak and over in seconds.

Shaye's thighs clamped closed around his ears as the first vicious convulsion seized her. She bucked, her hips undulating with each hard wave of release pushing her pussy harder against Coop's marauding mouth.

COOP COULDN'T GET ENOUGH. Not of her taste, her heat, her smell. Or the petal softness of the sweetest cunt he'd ever eaten. Shaye lived up to and beyond every carnal fantasy he'd conjured up in the last few months.

As she came down, he continued to lick and suck the throbbing flesh beneath his mouth. She was hot and wet and he wanted to drown in her.

The blast of a car horn acted like a slap to the face.

"Oh my God." Shaye's legs released their vice-like grip on his head and her hands pressed against his scalp as she tried to scramble away from him. "Cooper. Stop."

He lifted his head but didn't move from between her legs. "Easy, Shaye." Gliding his hands up and down her thighs, he said, "No one can see."

She tugged her skirt down to cover her, but his hands were in the way. "Move!"

Surging to his feet, Coop leaned into her—over her—his mouth a breath from hers. "No one can see."

"Only if they're blind."

"We're at the back of the lot and the truck door is between us and the world. They'd have to come right up and look over the damn thing or through the fucking windshield to see." He held her gaze with his. "And I'm not about to share you with anyone, so you can bet your sweet arse I'm not going to expose you."

"But—"

"No. Think about it, Shaye. At any point in the last few minutes have I not shielded your body with mine? Sure, it was obvious what we were doing, but at no time could anyone have seen any part of you that they wouldn't see if they'd been standing next to you inside the bar."

Coop watched her digest his words until he was satisfied she understood he'd never put her in such a vulnerable position.

"C'mon. Let's get out of here." He gripped her knees and swung her legs into the truck. Grabbing the seatbelt, Coop leaned in and clicked it into place.

He slammed the door with a little more force than necessary and made his way around to the driver's side. He knew he didn't have any real reason for his anger, but dammit, Shaye should know he'd never take a risk with her safety. Still fuming and not ready to say a word until he got his emotions under control, Coop jumped into the seat and jammed the key in the ignition.

Neither of them said a word as he drove away. He couldn't think of anything to defuse the tension, and the scent of sex and hot woman filling the cab didn't help him pull it together. He wasn't even going to think about the hard-on pressing against the zipper of his jeans.

"Where are we going?"

Coop took his eyes off the road for a second. "My place."

"What? No."

What the fuck was wrong with his place? "Ah, okay. Your place then."

"No."

"What the fuck?" He changed lanes and took the first side street they came to. Pulling over, he slammed the truck in park and turned to look at Shaye. "Care to enlighten me?"

"No hooking up at either of our houses."

"Hooking up?"

"Yeah. This." She waved a hand between them. "What we're doing. We need rules."

"Rules?" Coop's eyebrows rose. "You're fucking kidding, right?"

Shaye shook her head.

Jesus Christ, she was serious. He took a breath and tried to calm the riot of emotions going on inside him. He'd finally gotten his hands on her and she was still giving him the runaround. Something was up. Coop wasn't sure what, but he knew to his bones that there was a reason she was attempting to put parameters on what they were doing.

He'd get to the bottom of the problem one way or another, but for now, he'd let her have her way.

"Fine. What are your rules?"

3

SHAYE KNEW LAYING out boundaries might mean Coop would walk away, but if she didn't protect herself, she'd be going back to Perth with a broken heart. Taking a deep breath, she gave him her list.

"No hooking up at our places. No strings. No dating. And this is over in a month."

Coop eyed her for several long seconds. It took effort to keep breathing, to not hold her breath while she waited for him to say yes or no. She didn't count on him arguing.

"First, I want you in a bed. Preferably tied to it."

She shivered. Licked her lips. "Well, it won't be mine. Or yours."

"We'll see. Second, we're definitely not putting a time limit on this."

"But—"

"Nope. A month is not going to be enough time to get my fill of you." He leaned towards her. "And as for those strings, we're already so tangled in them neither of us are getting out any time soon."

"Coop—"

"No." He placed his finger against her lips. "You have your rules, I have mine. We're exclusive. While I'm fucking you, no one else is unless I invite them to share, and I have to tell you, Shaye, I'm so greedy for you that ain't ever gonna happen."

Air rushed through her parted lips. She wasn't sure if it was the idea of him sharing her or the fact he had no intention of it happening that had the flood of heat and moisture filling her pussy.

His eyes dilated, his nostrils flared. "Well, well. Seems that's a hot button. I'll have to see what I can do about that without bringing anyone into the bed we'll definitely find ourselves in."

"We're not—"

Coop laughed. "Yes, we are. And I know just where to find one." He closed the distance between them and slammed his mouth on hers.

Shaye had no time to react—no time to enjoy. Coop pulled his mouth from hers, a huge grin on his lips and put the truck in gear. He made a U-turn and had them back on the main road in seconds.

"Where are we going?" She seemed to be asking that question repeatedly, and it didn't escape her that she wasn't only referring to the physical direction they were taking.

"Bed." Coop glanced at her. "But don't worry. It's not mine or yours."

Was he taking her to a hotel? Did he want her that badly? Lord knows, she was desperate enough for him she'd pay hundreds of dollars for a few hours in a bed together. She just couldn't afford to let him into hers. And crawling into his would be far worse.

When Coop pulled into the driveway of a familiar two-story house, fear lodged in her throat. "This is—"

"Not anymore." He cut the engine. "I moved out six weeks ago. It sold yesterday but I haven't removed any of the furniture yet."

"Oh."

"You coming?" Coop opened his door and got out. Turning back, he said, "Dare you to."

She thought he'd come around to her side and get her. But he didn't. Instead, he walked toward the front door without looking back. Damn the man. Now she had to make the decision to take this where he obviously wanted it to go. Not that she didn't want it to go there too. She did. The quiver in her belly couldn't be ignored. Neither could the remembered pleasure or the slick heat throbbing in her pussy.

With every cell, she wanted more of what she'd had in the parking lot. So much more. And even with the threat to her heart, Shaye knew she wasn't going to turn him down. She couldn't walk away without knowing what it was like to have Cooper Moreland buried deep inside her.

COOP WASN'T A GAMBLER. He didn't leave things to chance. If he wanted something, he went after it, but sometimes you had to take a step away and let the cards fall where they would. Of course, he never did that without calculating all the outcomes—all the ways he could end up a loser. And he'd bet the 150 grand profit he'd made on flipping this house that Shaye would follow him inside.

There was no way she'd let him walk away. Still, he'd only give her five minutes, then he'd throw in the towel and go get her anyway. He was doing the right thing and giving her the choice. For now.

He left the door open behind him and headed for the second floor and the master bedroom with the king-size bed he'd brought in when he'd put the house up for sale. The bed not being his was a technicality, and he knew he was splitting hairs, but he hadn't slept in it even though he owned it.

The click of the front door closing echoed up the stairwell, and Coop resisted the urge to pump his fist in the air and yell *yes*. He used no restraint when it came to the smile on his lips though. That he let go until he figured he looked like the Cheshire cat.

Mentally running through what was in the house, he quickly worked out he didn't have anything on hand to tie her to the bed, so he'd have to improvise. He'd use his T-shirt to secure her hands to the headboard this first time.

Next time, he'd bind her spread-eagle.

He wasn't sure why he had such a strong desire to tie Shaye up. He'd tied women down before, but that had been a why-not impulse. Where the urge to have Shaye at his mercy was more a craving—a have-to-have-or-die need that scraped his bones and left him aching from head to toe.

Coop shook his head. She had him riding a razor edge in so many ways. He wanted her physically, there was no denying that, but he wanted more. He couldn't define what that more was except to say he wanted her to want him the same way. Needed her to.

"Cooper?" Shaye's voice echoing up from the ground floor snapped him out of his thoughts and reminded him of why he was there.

To have her on a bed.

"Up here." He threw the doors to the master suite open and headed straight for the bed. Toeing off his shoes as he whipped his T-shirt over his head, he contemplated stripping the bedcovers back or taking her on top. He'd leave them. The quicker he got naked, the quicker he could get Shaye naked and under him.

He tossed the shirt on the bed and reached for the button on his jeans. Coop had his pants undone and shoved past his knees when Shaye entered the room. She stopped short when her gaze landed on him. He didn't show any outward reaction, but the heat in her eyes, the rapid rise and fall of her chest and that tantalizing tongue of hers darting out to stroke over her bottom lip had his insides coiling tight.

Her eyes were wide, trained straight on the erection his boxer briefs couldn't hide. Stepping out of his jeans, he barely stopped himself from racing across the room and grabbing her. "You've got about thirty seconds to get out of those clothes or I'm ripping them off you."

Shaye jumped, her gaze darting up to his. "I...um..."

"Twenty-five."

She swept her tongue across her bottom lip again, and Coop couldn't hold back the moan.

"Ten."

"What?"

"Zero." He lunged for her.

"Cooper!"

He laughed at her indignant cry. "I warned you," he said as he pulled her into his arms.

"You either can't count, or you're a cheat."

"Let's get one thing straight right now. When it comes to you and getting you naked under me, all bets are off."

With that said, Coop gripped two handfuls of her skirt and yanked it down her legs. Next, he went after her top. She made a token effort to stop him, except all it took was one look in her eyes to know she was more than happy to let him strip her.

He stepped back to get a good look at her in nothing but her heels and red lace bra. Her underwear was still stuffed in his jeans pocket. He'd think about returning those later. Or not.

"Fuck. You're a wet dream," he growled.

Wrapping his hands around her waist, Coop picked her up and walked to the bed, where he tossed her into the middle. Not giving her time to get away, he crawled onto the bed and straddled her hips. "Do you trust me, Shaye?"

"Yes."

He loved that there was no hesitation. "Then put your arms above you head, wrists together."

Again, no hesitation, she just raised her arms and asked, "What are you going to do?"

"Tie you to the headboard." Coop grabbed his shirt and wrapped it around her wrists. "It's not the best, and it won't really hold you like I want, but it'll still give us both the desired effect."

"Okay."

"We won't really need a safe word as you'll be able to get loose easy enough, but pick one anyway. Make it memorable, because you'll use it every time from now on."

"E-every time?"

"Yeah." He'd played around with bondage a few times, and while his partners had always had safe words, they'd never needed them. With Shaye, it was different. He needed her to have one so he didn't go too far. His level of excitement was already off the charts, and he hadn't even secured her yet.

"Are you into BDSM?"

"No."

"But—"

"I need to know you're with me every second. If I do *anything* you don't like, say the word and I'll stop. No matter what."

"Taxi."

"Taxi?"

Shaye nodded, her teeth sinking into her bottom lip.

"Okay. Taxi."

Fuck. His hands were shaking. He hoped it was just the long months of anticipation that had him trembling like a virgin. Once he had her arms bound, he couldn't work out how to hook them to the bed. But maybe he didn't need to.

"I've changed my mind. Just keep your arms above you head unless I tell you otherwise." Sitting up, he took her in. The bra had to go.

It wasn't until he'd undone the rear clasp and tried to pull the straps off her arms that he realized his mistake. He should have thought about this before tying her up. Improvising —*again*—he pushed the bra up her arms and left it draped over his T-shirt. Her breathing had grown shallow and the short breaths made her breasts jiggle.

He filled his hands with her. Stroked his thumbs over her nipples while squeezing, pushing her generous tits together to form a deep cleavage that he couldn't wait to slide his cock through.

"Do you have any idea how long I've wanted to get my hands on these tits?" Coop used his thumbs and index fingers to pinch the extended tips. "You gonna let me fuck them, Shaye? Let me slide my cock in between until I come all over your chest?"

She arched into his touch, her teeth scraping at the plump flesh of her bottom lip. The provocative move sent a shaft of lust through his balls, and Coop had to bite the inside of his cheek to keep from jumping her right then. He wanted to play first. See what she liked and what she didn't.

"Don't move." He hopped off the bed and stripped out of his underwear. Grabbing his jeans, he dug in his pocket for his wallet and the two condoms he kept tucked inside. Protection in hand, Coop climbed back onto the bed and kneeled beside her. "Now. Where was I?"

. . .

SHAYE COULDN'T CATCH her breath. For what felt like a hundred years—but could only be a few minutes—Coop had been torturing her with his hands and mouth—his body. He'd even used his cock—rubbing, pressing and dragging it over sensitive flesh to tease her until she was on the verge of going insane. Hell, she was already there. Why else would she want to beg him to stop and never stop in the same breath?

"Cooper." She licked her dry lips. "Please."

"What? Tell me what you want."

He spoke against her stomach, his breath shivering over her skin. He'd been using his lips, tongue and teeth to send her out of her mind with anticipation, and she'd finally had enough. Now she'd beg.

"More." She thrust her hips off the bed to clue him in to where she wanted him to go next. "Lower."

"Where? Here?" He trailed his mouth over her hipbone and down her outer thigh.

"No." Shaye spread her legs.

"Tell me." Coop scraped his teeth along her leg towards her pussy. "I want to hear you say it."

"Yes." Her hips bucked. "There. Right there."

"Say it," he growled, hovering his mouth over her throbbing sex.

"Lick me."

"Words, Shaye. Tell me *what* to lick."

God. His mouth was so close she could feel the moist heat of his breath. "Pussy. Lick my pussy. My clit." She panted.

"There now. That wasn't so hard, was it?" He blew a hot stream of air over her.

She shuddered. "Please." He still hadn't touched her, and she brought her bound hands down to grip his head and push him against her throbbing pussy. "Cooper. Please."

"Hands back over your head."

The command snapped out at her, Coop's voice raw—harsh. Without thought, Shaye immediately returned her arms to their previous position.

"Good girl."

She knew she should take offence. Should be insulted by his tone, but she had no chance to think when Coop finally did what she'd been begging for.

He spread her open with his thumbs and zeroed in on her clit. He laved her with his tongue, wrapped his lips around the hard knot of nerves and sucked.

Her back bowed, her hips driving her pussy into his mouth as an orgasm tore through her. It was unexpected and ripped a scream of pleasure from her throat. Body thrashing, Shaye surrendered to the blinding release.

Coop didn't let her come down. He kept at her, with fingers and mouth and tongue, he drove her straight into a second climax. This one left her a trembling, sated puddle of goo on the bed beneath him.

Shaye's arms were still above her head and her legs spread wide when Coop crawled up over her and settled between her thighs.

"I wanna see you do that again." He nudged his cock against her quivering pussy. "But this time, I'm gonna be buried deep when you give me what I want."

She shivered as he ran his hands up her extended arms and curled his fingers around hers. Using what little strength she had, Shaye opened her eyes and met Cooper's gaze.

"There you are." He rocked his hips, sliding his cock through her slick folds. "I was wondering if maybe you'd passed out."

His gloating was obvious, and Shaye should really shoot some holes in that monumental ego of his, but she didn't have a smartass comment. And even if she did, she wasn't sure she wanted to risk him stopping now. A softly hummed murmur was all she could manage anyway.

He grinned. "Not out, but delirious with pleasure."

Oh, yeah, he needed that ego shot down. "Not yet. You mustn't be trying hard enough."

Coop flexed his hips. "We'll have to rectify that."

"Bring it—" Her reply turned into a moan, because in one hard thrust, Coop buried himself inside her.

4

COOPER GROANED. He'd died and gone to heaven. It was the only explanation. Nothing on earth should feel this good. He lowered his head and nuzzled Shaye's neck. Flexing his hips, he withdrew his cock until only the head remained lodged inside her tight cunt.

The moan that slipped through her lips along with the soft walls surrounding his sensitive crown had him pushing back in. Unlike the first time he drove into her, he took this plunge slowly, pressing forward at an agonizing pace that delivered sensations so sublime they bordered on pain.

"So tight." He pulled out. Thrust back in. "Hot, wet, tight."

Shaye wrapped her legs around his hips and rocked up into him. It was all he needed to tip him over the edge of civil straight into savage.

He rose up on his forearms and knees, bracing his weight and using the bed to get the power he needed to fuck her. Hard.

Glancing down, he watched Shaye's eyes glaze over as he drove into her over and over. He tilted his hips to change the angle of entry and was rewarded with a cry of pleasure when he ground his pelvis against her clit on each down stroke.

Her cunt walls closed around him, sucking at his length as he forged through the swollen tissues. She tightened with each lunge. Cried out with every beat of his body on hers.

Coop shuddered. The pace—the pleasure—had his orgasm only strokes away. But before he let himself go, he wanted to feel Shaye come on his cock. Lifting up on one arm, he slid the other one between them and found her clit with his fingers. He pressed. Circled. Pressed. Matched the speed with his thrusts. Increased the pressure and had her writhing under him.

But it wasn't enough. She fought it. Fought him. And he wasn't having it. He'd take nothing less than everything he wanted from her and what he wanted was to send her flying once more.

"C'mon, Shaye, let go." He slammed into her harder. "Come for me. Come *on* me."

She broke. Clamped around him with such brutal force his movements slowed, the drag of his cock through her clenching cunt harder than before—the squeeze on his shaft greater. Her cry echoed in the room around them and merged with his groan as he let himself follow her into the ecstasy swallowing them whole.

He collapsed on top of her, managed to get his elbows locked so he didn't crush her beneath him. As it was, a good part of his weight held her hips pinned to the bed.

"Give me a second and I'll get off you," he murmured against her throat.

Her only reply was to tighten her legs around him.

Coop loved that she didn't want to let him go. He didn't want to examine how much. Not yet. Besides, he was pretty sure once the euphoria of her climax faded, Shaye would be shoving him away. Physically and emotionally.

He had no idea why she'd insisted on having rules, but Coop was one hundred percent sure he was plowing straight through every one of them. After finally getting inside her, there was no doubt she was what he wanted. And not just for the next month.

The honest, *mind-blowing* truth was he wanted Shaye Adams for the rest of his life.

DID she think she was in trouble?

Hell yes.

Trouble didn't even begin to cover what she was. Her rules weren't going to save her from heartache. It was already too late. Probably had been long before she'd started flirting with the man she'd lusted after for eight years.

She was so stupid.

Shaye squeezed her eyes closed and hoped she could hide her feelings from Cooper. The last thing she wanted was for him to know how into him she was. Sex was one thing, but handing him her heart along with her body wasn't something she was prepared to do. He'd proven over the years that no woman could hold his interest, and Shaye had no desire to be one of the many broken hearts he left behind.

"Need to get rid of the condom." Coop pulled away, a shudder wracking them both as his softening cock slipped from her body.

He untangled the T-shirt from her arms before he rolled off the bed. Shaye couldn't help but watch his naked arse as he walked towards the bathroom. She wanted him now more than she had earlier. That knowledge had her leaping off the bed and scrambling for her clothes.

She'd be a fool to stick around any longer. Her defenses needed fortifying. There was no way she could let him touch her again until she'd done some damage control—slapped a few more bricks in those walls.

"What are you doing?"

Shaye glanced up as she hooked her bra together. "Dressing?"

"Why?"

"Well, I can't go home naked." She wiggled into her skirt.

He narrowed his eyes and fisted his hands at his sides. "So what? You're just gonna fuck and run?"

She froze. How could she answer that without raising a red flag, when technically she *was* running? "That's a little crude."

"Crude or truth?" One thick eyebrow arched and his eyes sparked with challenge.

Avoiding his gaze, she glanced around looking for her top. "I need to be up early tomorrow."

He came closer, stopping with his feet inches from hers, the heat from his naked body caressing her through her clothes. "I'm not done with you."

Before Shaye could take a breath, she was in his arms, her mouth crushed beneath his. He wasn't gentle. He demanded. He took. He conquered. The thrust of his tongue was over-whelming in its ferocity—obliterating everything from her mind except him. And when he walked her backwards and pushed her onto the bed, she didn't argue.

Couldn't.

Not when his hand was between her legs, his talented fingers strumming her clit until she gasped for breath as he ruthlessly drove her towards another orgasm.

The climax hit her fast and hard. Shattered her. Mind, body, soul. It was mind numbing. Cooper destroyed all resis-tance—every barrier—until she had no choice but to surrender completely.

Spent, Shaye lay sprawled on the bed, her eyelids too heavy

to lift, her lungs too weak to breath. She heard the tear of foil. Felt his strong fingers dig into her hips.

"Nowhere near done."

Shaye's head spun when he flipped her over and raised her hips. His hands smoothed up the back of her thighs, pushing her skirt up, up, up. He palmed her arse cheeks, slipping his thumbs between to find her slick heat and tease her with barely there caresses.

"Cooper." She arched her back, pushed her arse towards him.

He chuckled. "Yeah. We're so not done."

He pushed his knee between hers, forcing her legs wider, making her arch deeper, thrusting her arse higher. She felt the tip of his cock at her entrance a split second before he drove his length inside her.

A cry burst from her throat, Cooper's groan rumbled in her ear as he curled over her, his chest to her back. She thought he'd take her hard. Fast. Instead, she got slow and easy strokes while his mouth explored the sensitive skin beneath her ear.

Her body strained against his. She rocked as best she could beneath him, but he'd caged her in. Held her captive to his gentle thrusts—hostage to the flood of sensation—to the waves of pleasure swamping her. To him.

Whatever he asked, she'd do. Whatever he demanded, she'd give. In that moment, she could do nothing but accept the feelings bursting free inside her. With Cooper's hands caressing her breasts, his lips fluttering over her skin, words of pleasure—of approval—whispered in her ear and the slow, steady drive of his body against hers, she surrendered. As her orgasm tore through her and Coop came right along with her, Shaye had no hope of shielding her heart.

· · ·

COOP PICKED up his shirt without taking his eyes off the bathroom door. Shaye had barely waited for him to roll off her before she'd scrambled out of bed, grabbed her clothes and made a beeline for the bathroom. He had to assume they were done for the night. Especially seeing how he'd persuaded her into a second round—not that she'd protested after he'd gotten his hands and mouth on her.

He wasn't sure what to make of her reactions. She seemed completely into him, seemed as desperate for him as he was for her, then it was like a sudden wind change. Gone was the hot blast of need, replaced by an arctic cold shoulder.

Shaking his head as he finished dressing, Coop wondered if Shaye would continue to blow hot and cold now they'd moved past friends to lovers. The thought didn't sit well. A lead ball sank to the pit of his stomach, a tight vice squeezed his chest and a red haze filled his vision.

He'd be fucked if he'd let her back away now.

The question was how to handle her from here. Other than her *rules*, they hadn't really discussed what it was they wanted or expected. Not that he had a clue himself. Well, not beyond the bone-deep need he had for her. He had to come up with a plan.

One that kept her close but didn't freak her out. Why he thought Shaye feared getting close was anyone's guess, but Coop knew, like he knew her eyes were blue, that she wanted to keep an emotional distance between them. And the more he thought about it, the more he was convinced she was playing him. He hadn't a clue how or why, he just couldn't shake the gut-sure notion that he was being played.

Two could play that game. He knew what his goal was. He only had to figure out Shaye's before she made her final move.

Coop figured he was a sick bastard, but he couldn't deny the anticipation thrumming in his veins. He'd never encountered a woman who challenged him, teased him—tempted—drew a need to control so sharp it sliced through him and sucked the breath from his lungs.

"Ready?"

He glanced up to see Shaye—worse luck, fully clothed—standing before him. "Sure."

"Let's go then." She strode past him and out the door.

Right. The arctic freeze was back. Taking a deep breath, he turned and followed her. Shaye was at the bottom by the time he hit the top of the staircase.

In a hurry much?

Coop smiled. She was running again.

He wanted to laugh but stifled the urge. Pissing her off wouldn't get him what he wanted. And what he wanted was to see Shaye running towards him instead of away. She'd given him a month. Thirty days to play out this thing between them. Except Coop figured they could tangle for the next hundred years and what was arcing between them wouldn't be finished. All he had to do was convince Shaye what they had shouldn't have a time limit.

Easier said than done.

When he made it to the open front door, he could see her waiting on the passenger side of his truck. She really did want to get out of there. With a sigh, he locked up and headed in her direction. Clicking the fob to unlock the doors, he watched her climb in and buckle up before he'd even made it to the driver's door.

Yep. She wanted gone. Now.

Too bad he wasn't playing by her rules.

"Where to?" he asked as he slid into his seat.

"Home."

"Yours?"

She finally looked at him. "Of course. Who else's?"

He grinned. Coop knew he was about to poke the sleeping bear, but he couldn't help himself. "Thought you might have changed your mind and wanted to head to my place."

Her mouth dropped open. Closed. Opened. She licked her bottom lip and sucked in a breath. "No. No hooking up at each other's houses. Remember?"

"Oh, I remember everything you've said." Coop shoved the key in the ignition and fired up the engine. "But fair warning, Shaye. I plan to break every one of those rules."

Giving her no opportunity to argue, he put the truck in reverse and turned up the radio. Let her stew on that while he drove her home. She might think she had him by the balls—and while the idea of her holding that particular part of his anatomy had said anatomy drawing tight—he wasn't going to let her lead him around by them.

The drive was quiet except for the hard beat of rock music filling the cab. The tension between them ratcheted up with every kilometre of road he drove over, and he figured she'd be ready to explode when they reached her house. But when he pulled into her driveway, Shaye had her belt off and her door open before he'd set the handbrake.

He couldn't stop the laughter when she leapt out, slammed the door behind her and all but ran towards her front door. She wasn't getting rid of him that easily.

Knowing he couldn't waste a second, Coop left the truck running and climbed out. Jogging, he hit the front porch just as Shaye swung the door open. She flicked on the inside light and he froze.

"What the fuck?"

Shaye spun around with a hand on her chest. "Cooper."

Why was she so surprised to see him standing there? "Who else? What's with all the boxes?" He gestured to the pile stacked along the hall wall.

"Oh. Um. I'm moving."

His gaze darted to hers. "What? Why? Where?"

"The temp jobs I'm managing to pick up aren't enough for me to keep living here." She stepped through the doorway and moved to close the door.

No invitation to come inside and she'd only answered one of his questions. "Where are you moving to?" He closed the distance between them.

"I...um..." She licked her lips and Coop's insides clenched. "Somewhere smaller. Cheaper."

Coop moved closer, crowding her farther inside and getting one foot in the doorway so she couldn't shut the door in his face like he knew she wanted to. "I get that. But where?"

She avoided his gaze, shifted on her feet. "I, well, I'm still looking."

"You're packing without having somewhere to go?" Something else was going on. He hadn't a clue what, but she was being too evasive, too...secretive.

"I'm saving time. Plus, I'll be downsizing, so I'm getting rid of stuff as well." She'd found some of her usual confidence, but Coop still wasn't buying whatever she was selling.

He moved into her personal space, brought his face inches from hers. "I don't know what's really going on or why you're not telling me, but I can guarantee you I'll find out what you're hiding."

Shaye stepped back, putting a couple of feet between them. "I'm not hiding anything."

Coop grinned. "Sure you are."

She gasped, but before she could get a word out, he'd moved in and crushed her mouth beneath his.

He meant to be quick. Meant to leave her hanging—craving more. But the second his tongue slipped between her lips, he was lost.

Her mouth was hot and wet and reminded him of all he'd done tonight. All he still wanted to do. He slid his hands up her back. Down. Gripped her arse and pulled her closer until they touched from chest to thigh. A groan rumbled in his throat while Shaye whimpered and moaned, rocked her softness against him, and he knew if he didn't back out now, he'd have her here.

Tearing his mouth from hers, Coop tried to suck in breath. "We aren't done. And you *will* tell me what the fuck is going on."

Before she could say something he'd regret. Before he could push her against the wall and do all the dirty things his body wanted, he spun around and leapt down the two steps.

He had to leave. Needed to clear his head to think, and there was no doing that if he could see her. She scrambled his brains and sent his libido into overdrive. The only thing he could think about when he was around her was fucking her senseless, and that wouldn't get him the plan he needed to smash through her stupid rules and convince her he—they— were worth more than a short-lived affair.

5

PHONE TO HIS EAR, Cooper paced his living room. This was the second call he'd made and still no one was answering.

He was about to hang up when Kelsey's sleep-fogged voice filled his ear. "Hello?"

"Did you know Shaye was moving?" he growled.

"Coop?"

He could hear movement, sheets rustling, someone grumbling, and he assumed he'd woken her up. Which explained why West hadn't answered his phone when Coop had rung two minutes ago. He sighed. "Yeah."

"Do you know what time it is?"

Coop ran a hand down his face and sighed again. 5:30 a.m. "Sorry. I left it as late as I could. She's got boxes stacked up by her front door." He didn't understand the fear eating at his gut. Didn't know why a few packing boxes would have him walking the floor all night.

"Who? Shaye?" Kelsey asked.

"Yes. And she won't tell me where she's moving to."

"O-okay." There was move rustling before Kelsey said, "What exactly did she say?"

"She can't afford to stay where she is—"

"That makes sense. She's already sold her car."

"Sold her car?" He didn't mean to yell, but that piece of news didn't make him feel any better than the sight of those boxes. Shaye loved that car. "When?"

"A few weeks ago." Kelsey's sigh travelled down the line and into his ear. "You know she still hasn't found a permanent job, and those temp ones might pay well, but they don't last long, and she's having more days without earning income than with to afford the fancy car or the big house."

"I get that. But something isn't right."

"Cooper."

"No. Listen to me. She was cagey, hesitating over her words like she didn't know what to say. She's hiding something, I know it." He scrubbed a hand over his face again. "I can't explain it, Kelsey, I just know she's being secretive in a way I've never known her to be."

"Fine. I'm meeting her for lunch later. I'll see if I can find out anything."

Coop could hear the skepticism in her voice but chose to ignore it. "Thanks. Is West working while you're out?" He knew his best friend had cut back on the hours he worked on weekends since he and Kelsey got married.

"No. He'll be here."

"I'll come over and keep him company then." He could wait for Kelsey to return with the answers Shaye hadn't given him.

"Cooper, what's going on?"

"That's what I want to know."

"No. I mean with you. Why the sudden curiosity about what Shaye's up to?"

"It's not sudden." Jesus. They'd been discussing the situation between him and Shaye just last night at the club.

"Okay, granted, your interest might not be new, but this intensity is."

He didn't want to get into this with Shaye's best friend. Coop might have known Kelsey since high school, and she was married to his best friend, but he didn't delude himself as to where her loyalties would lie.

Girlfriends stuck together. Especially when the male gender was involved.

"Cooper?"

"What?" He could hear a lecture coming on.

"Don't fuck with her. She's been through enough lately."

"I'm not going to fuck with her." Not the way Kelsey was talking about anyway. He had every intention of *fucking* Shaye again, but he didn't think he had the power to hurt her the way Kelsey was implying. Shaye, on the other hand, had dug so deep beneath his skin, she'd soaked into his bone marrow. If anyone was going to be left bruised from them hooking up, it would be him.

Kelsey sighed and he could picture her shaking her head. "You don't have a clue, do you?"

"About what?"

"Oh, no, I'm not telling you. It'll be more fun to watch you work it out on your own."

Kelsey hung up, giving him no opportunity to question her further.

It didn't matter.

All he needed to know was what was going on with Shaye.

"YOU CAN'T KEEP it from me forever," Kelsey said.

Shaye looked across the table at her best friend. "Keep

what?" She'd stall as long as she could. She didn't want to have this conversation.

Kelsey arched one eyebrow, the look Shaye had been on the receiving end of numerous times.

She hadn't told Kelsey about the job offer. It was a dream job. One anybody in Shaye's position would jump at. One Shaye had worked her whole life to get. "I got offered a full-time job. Director of accounts."

"Oh my God! That's fantastic." Kelsey launched out of her seat and came around the table. She wrapped Shaye in a hug and rocked back and forth. "Yay, yay, yay!"

"Jeez, settle down. It's just a job." Shaye noticed those around them looking with curiosity.

Kelsey let her go and re-took her seat. She picked up her phone and started to tap away at the screen. "We have to celebrate."

"What? No. I don't want anyone to know yet." Shaye reached across and put her hand over Kelsey's.

Cocking her head to the side, Kelsey asked, "Why not?"

There was no putting it off. "It's in Perth."

"What is?"

"The job."

Kelsey sat up straight, her eyes wide, mouth turned down. "You're moving back to Perth?"

"That's where the job is." Shaye hadn't accepted the offer yet, but it was a dream job. She'd be stupid not to take it. "I've spent years working towards this type of position."

And she had. She should be excited. Should have already said yes and booked her flight and the movers. But like this conversation with her best friend, she'd been putting all those things off.

"If it's what you've wanted for years, why don't you look happy?" Kelsey asked.

Trust Kelsey to read between the lines. Shaye shrugged. "It's in Perth."

"Your family's there. You grew up there."

"Yes. But you know I'm not close with my sister or brother. And Mum and Dad have always been too busy living their lives to worry about their children." Not that her parents had been neglectful or abusive. They just weren't overly attentive or affectionate. More often than not, they were just uninterested.

Since moving to Sydney, Shaye hadn't seen them, was lucky to speak to them four times a year—Christmas and birthdays. And even those weren't guaranteed.

Kelsey was eyeing Shaye in a way that had her squirming in her chair. She could almost hear the wheels spinning in her friend's head.

"What?" Shaye asked as she picked up her coffee.

With a smug grin, Kelsey leaned forward and declared, "You had sex with Cooper."

Shaye choked, the sip she hadn't quite swallowed hit reverse and came out her nose and mouth in a good imitation of a high-pressure hose. Grabbing a handful of serviettes, Shaye mopped up as best she could. She'd have to go straight home and soak her shirt. It was one of her favorites and now sported a big splash of brown down the front.

"Dammit. This'll never come out." She scrubbed at the large spot.

Kelsey reached across with her glass of water. "Here. Dab the serviettes in this. Try sponging it out with the water."

Shaye eyed her dubiously but took the glass and did as suggested. Surprisingly, the stain began to fade a little. "Hey, this might work."

"Make sure you wash it in cold water. Hot will set the stain." Kelsey raised her hand to signal the waitress. "I'll get the check."

"No. We'll split it."

Kelsey shook her head. "Nope. This one's on me. You get the next."

Shaye knew what Kelsey was doing and she appreciated the thought. It still irked though. She hated being short on funds, but there was no denying she was. If she didn't accept the job soon, she'd be forced to dip deeper into her savings, something she wanted to avoid at all costs.

She tried to smile. "Thanks."

Kelsey grinned. "You're welcome."

Shaye would make sure she returned the favour next time. Job or no job.

"Okay. So when's the big move?" Kelsey asked.

Shaye's stomach cramped. The mango salad she'd eaten churned. Why did the thought of moving back to Perth make her feel sick? The salary alone should have her jumping for joy.

But she wasn't.

Nothing about the offer improved her current state of anxiety. It only added to it. She couldn't put off answering Kelsey. Not like she'd been putting off the woman from the employment agency.

"It's a new year start."

"Wow. That's months away." Kelsey handed her credit card to the waitress. "So you'll have time to settle in over there before you start."

She wouldn't be starting if she didn't accept the job soon. She had until November ten. Less than two weeks to decide. "Depends on when I pull up stakes here."

Kelsey leaned over and placed her hand on Shaye's. "What's wrong? You don't look happy, and for a dream job, you're certainly lacking in excitement."

Shaye shrugged. "Perth is no longer home."

"I get that. You've made some ties here, but they aren't family."

"They're closer than the people that are my family."

"Does it have anything to do with you finally hooking up with Coop?"

Ah, back to that. She should have known Kelsey wouldn't let that topic die. Shaye frowned. "Hooking up doesn't imply attachment."

Kelsey laughed.

Shaye's frown grew. "I fail to see what's funny." She folded her arms over her chest.

"You are. He is." She spoke through her laughter. "God, you two have danced around each other for months, and I *know* you've had a thing for him from the beginning."

"I have not!"

Kelsey arched one of her eyebrows.

"Okay, fine. I've had a *little* thing for Coop for a while." Shaye held up her hand with her thumb and finger a few millimetres apart.

That only sent Kelsey into another fit of laughter.

"Whatever." Shaye grabbed her handbag. "Let's get out of here."

"Why don't we head back to my place? You can help me pick out a colour for my office."

Shaye glanced at Kelsey. "Didn't we do that the other week?"

Kelsey ducked her head. "Yeah."

"Explain."

"It's not the same on the walls as it was on the paint card."

"Oh my God. You're going to make West repaint the room, aren't you?"

Kelsey glared. "It's too bright. I have to wear my sunglasses just to look in there."

Shaye didn't believe for one minute that it was that bad. "Can we swing by my place first so I can soak this shirt and grab a clean one?"

"That's fifteen minutes out of our way. I'll lend you something."

Kelsey didn't wait for her to agree before plucking her card and receipt out of the waitress's hand and heading out. Shaye followed behind after checking neither of them had left anything on or under the table. She wasn't sure she was in the mood to spend the afternoon with friends she'd have to say goodbye to soon.

For weeks, every time Shaye had seen one of their group, she'd wanted to cry. She was leaving them behind—walking away from the life she'd lived for the past eight years—and moving back to Perth. And telling Kelsey about the job offer hadn't made it any easier to accept.

COOP STOPPED mid sip when Shaye walked into West's kitchen. He hadn't expected to see her. Wasn't sure which emotion was the strongest, but the sight of her had dread and anticipation thrumming through him.

She was wearing another of those sexy short skirts, leaving miles of leg on full display, and he was a guy, so he looked. Once he got his fill of those, his gaze moved on up her torso to the tight tank top she wore. And the large stain right smack in between her glorious boobs.

He was definitely looking now.

"Ahem."

His gaze darted over to meet Kelsey's. "Hey, Coop. Didn't know you were coming over." The grin on her face said otherwise. Not to mention he'd told her he'd be here.

What game was she playing? He smiled. If she wanted to

pretend they hadn't spoken earlier, he was good with that. "So what have you two been up to?"

"Lunch and gossip," Kelsey said as she passed by on her way to West. She gave his best friend a kiss that really needed a room, but Coop figured it was their house, so he looked away.

Unfortunately—or fortunately—his gaze landed right back on Shaye's tits. "Looks like you wore lunch instead of eating it."

Shaye quickly crossed her arms over her chest, obscuring his view, but it was too late. He already knew what was under there. And he couldn't wait to get his mouth and hands on them again.

"Oh. We need to wash that top." Kelsey—no longer sucking face with West—grabbed Shaye's wrist and pulled her from the room. "We'll be back," she tossed over her shoulder.

"You want a cloth for that drool?"

Coop spun to face West. It was hard when the sexy sway of Shaye's arse held his attention, but he managed. Barely. "Huh?"

"The drool? On your chin?" West tipped his head in the direction the girls had gone.

Ah. Right. "Funny." Cooper took a swig of beer.

"So what gives?"

"Nothing."

West chuckled. "Yep. Sure. I see that."

"How did you see anything? You were too busy sticking your tongue down Kelsey's throat."

West's grin grew. "So what gives?"

Coop scowled.

"C'mon man. You undressed her and fucked her on my kitchen counter with your eyes. Don't you dare tell me nothing."

Well, there was no disputing that. Coop was pretty sure

that's exactly what his eyes had done. He sighed. "We fucked last night."

"About time."

"Yeah. Okay, it is, but she's put all these rules on us hooking up." Coop ran a hand over his jaw. "They're bullshit."

"So? I've never known you to worry about rules, especially bullshit ones." West opened the fridge and grabbed another two beers.

Coop shook his head. "Not for me. I'm driving."

West put the extra one back and cracked the top on his. "What's the plan?"

"What makes you think I've got a plan?"

"The last twenty-odd years as your friend."

Coop couldn't deny that. Cooper, West and Zac, Cooper's twin, had made up a trio since their first day of school. During their high school years, Zac and West had grown closer, but since leaving school, the three of them had gotten back to the way they'd been as little boys. Tight.

He finished off his beer and dropped the bottle in the bin before answering. It gave him a few seconds to work things out in his head. Not that it helped. "I don't have one other than using the off-the-charts chemistry we've got going on."

West shrugged. "Whatever works. But Shaye doesn't seem the type to fall into line easy."

"No. Take last night. She was out of bed and running the second I pulled out."

"Running? That isn't the Shaye I know." West frowned.

"I know, right? There has to be something going on. Something other than her lack of a job."

"There is," Kelsey said behind him.

6

"SAY THAT AGAIN." Coop couldn't have heard Kelsey right.

"The job is in Perth."

"Perth? As in, on the other side of Australia from Sydney, Perth?"

Kelsey nodded.

"No fucking way." Shaye was not moving. There was no way she'd start something with him then...oh fuck. That little... "Where is she?"

"What?" Kelsey asked, confusion all over her face.

"Where is she? Right now. Where?" He started across the kitchen.

"In the bathroom getting cha—"

He didn't wait for Kelsey to finish talking. His long legs ate up the distance in seconds and, without knocking, Coop turned the handle and entered the bathroom.

"Argh. Cooper!"

He shut the door behind him. Flicked the lock.

"What are you doing?" Her angry words and fierce glare

were negated by the fact his brain wasn't registering anything but the tits on display in front of him.

She was wearing some white lacy thing that pushed her boobs up and in. Damn. There was a lot of flesh on show. Coop took a step closer.

"Don't you dare come near me." Shaye held out a hand, palm out, the other one she splayed over her chest as though she thought it covered her. Ha. A sack couldn't cover those beauties.

Coop grinned and kept moving closer. There was no unseeing what had been seen.

"Cooper." His chest came in contact with Shaye's outstretched hand. "I'm trying to get dressed."

"I'd rather you get undressed."

Shaye's glare turned so deadly it was a wonder he was still standing.

Pushing against her hand, he waited for her to give. It didn't take long. Her elbow bent and he closed the distance between them, trapping her hand between his chest and her tits. He wrapped his arms around her and palmed her lower back. Sliding his hands north, he said, "Let me help you."

With a practiced flick of his fingers, he had Shaye's bra undone.

"W-what are you doing?"

"Helping."

"That isn't helping." She wiggled in his arms, but he wasn't letting go of her any time soon.

"Yes, it is." Coop trailed his fingers up her shoulder blades to her shoulders. "I'll show you how much it helps."

To stop any further argument, Coop lowered his head and took her mouth with his. There was a muffled squeak—of surprise, not protest.

And then she moved with him. She thrust her tongue

against his as he dove deeper. He groaned into her mouth when she slid her hands into his hair and tugged. Not one to miss an opportunity, Coop let his own hands roam.

First, he skimmed her bra straps off her shoulders. Then he dragged his fingertips up the slope of her neck until he cradled her face in his hands. He eased back on the kiss, sucked in a breath and tried to gather his wits.

"You fuck with my head." Coop pressed his forehead to Shaye's. "I didn't come in here for this. But I'll be fucked if I'm letting this chance to get inside you again go."

He dropped to his knees and went to work on her skirt. Whoever invented these stretchy no-zip skirts was a genius. In a second, he had it around her ankles.

"Cooper."

Ignoring Shaye's half-arsed protest, he leaned in and placed his mouth over her cunt through her undies and sucked.

She dug her nails into his shoulders but didn't push him away. She pulled him closer.

It was going to be hard and fast. For both of them.

Coop worked her with his tongue. With one hand, he popped the button on his pants and the other he used to palm her arse and pull her closer.

He could taste her through the cloth. Feel the heat of her on his tongue. She rocked against him and he didn't need to look up to know she had her lip caught between her teeth, stifling her moans. Once Shaye got going, there was no stopping her from taking what she wanted.

And she wanted to come.

It was in the way she moved. The way she tangled her fingers in his hair. Her murmured words for more.

He tugged on his zipper and freed his cock. Then, gripping the flimsy sides of her undies he yanked them down her legs.

Coop glanced up and met her lust-dazed eyes. "From behind or ride?"

"Huh?"

"Ride it is."

Coop grabbed her hips and urged her down. She straddled him. Pressed close. Her hot cunt coated his cock in her juices. Moaning, Shaye rocked her clit against him.

"Guide me in," he directed as he lifted her from his lap.

Her hand was warm and tight around him, but that was nothing compared to the hot grip of her cunt a second later when she plunged down and took him all the way in.

This time, they both moaned. The sound echoed around them, and Coop knew there was no way Kelsey and West wouldn't know what they were doing.

He should be ashamed. Should probably stop. Except there was no stopping when he was buried deep inside Shaye. Nothing short of death would get him to quit now.

Flexing his hips, he thrust up into her while using his hands on her hips to pull her down. She soon caught his rhythm and they were panting and moaning and rocking and sweating and climbing towards release so fucking fast his brain was spinning.

"Cooper." She grabbed his head and shoved him face first into her tits. "Suck my nipple. I'm so close."

There was no need to tell him twice. He opened his mouth and rooted around like a blind man until he had a taut peak between his lips. Then he sucked.

Hard.

He used his teeth to pinch the puckered flesh, to hold it in place so he could lash it with his tongue.

That was when things got wild.

She rode him like he'd never been ridden before. Up and down. Squeeze and release. Shaye worked his body with hers as though she'd been doing it for years. As though she knew every little thing that drove him crazy and used it.

His balls tightened. Blood pounded. And a split second after Shaye cried out Coop followed her into ecstasy.

SHAYE SLUMPED FORWARD. Coop's arms were wrapped around her and his cock was buried in her pussy, and for the life of her she couldn't work out how they'd ended up in this position.

On Kelsey's bathroom floor.

Half naked.

Fucked senseless.

She remembered protesting. Remembered telling him...

God. She didn't remember anything after he'd put his hands on her.

The man was lethal.

And turning her into a nymphomaniac.

Because even though neither of them had caught their breath and he was still buried inside her, she wanted him again. And that was why she needed to leave. Now.

"I have to go," she murmured against his neck but didn't move.

"Mmm." Coop's hands swept up and down her back. "Not yet."

"I can't believe we just did that. In Kelsey's bathroom."

"I can."

"You can?" She really had to leave. Except her body wasn't on the same page as her brain.

"Yeah. Just looking at you gets me hard. Touching you guarantees I'm getting inside you. Regardless of where we are."

"Then you can't touch me. Or see me." Shaye still hadn't crawled out of Coop's lap.

He laughed. "That's not going to happen."

Shaye sighed. Cooper was right. It didn't matter that she was leaving or that it was inevitable that he'd break her heart. She wasn't walking away from this any time soon. "We should get dressed before Kelsey or West come looking for us."

"Give it another minute." He tightened his arms.

"We don't have a minute. Kelsey will be knocking on the door any second." Shaye finally managed to get enough energy to lift off Cooper.

Muscles protested and sparks of pleasure darted through her pussy when his cock slipped free. The urge to plunge back down—to take him deep again—slashed through her, but she grit her teeth and pushed to her feet.

He kneeled between her legs, his cock hard and standing tall in spite of his recent orgasm. Coop's thick shaft was wet with their combined fluids and—

"Oh shit."

Coop steadied her with his hands on her hips. "What?"

"We didn't use protection."

"I. Fuck. I'm sorry. I didn't even think of it. I'm clean."

Shaye looked at him, saw the genuine remorse in his eyes and figured it wasn't something he did often. "That's not what I'm worried about."

"Are you on the pill?"

"No." She shook her head. When was her last period? Three weeks ago? Two?

"I've never forgotten before." Cooper got to his feet. "You scramble my brain every time I get near you, but that's no excuse. Whatever happens, I'll stand up."

"I know that." Shaye looked around for her clothes. How she'd ended up completely naked while he'd only undone his pants was a mystery. Although she had to admit it was hot. Her body still hummed with arousal—still craved Cooper's hands, his cock.

"Shaye." He waited for her to meet his gaze. "Whatever happens I'm here."

Their gazes remained locked for long seconds before Shaye nodded and looked away. "I know."

"Here." Coop held out her undies.

"Thanks." She took her underwear and slipped them on. Next, he handed over her skirt. Then her bra. The shirt she'd borrowed to replace her stained one was still sitting on the counter where she'd put it. "You should go out first so they don't see us leave together."

"I don't think it matters. West and Kelsey aren't stupid. They have to know we're in here together." Coop had cleaned up and fixed his clothes and now leaned against the door in a sexy pose that had her pussy clenching. "I'll wait for you."

She wanted to argue. Needed a few moments to herself to work through what they'd done. And she wasn't talking about having sex in her best friend's bathroom.

They'd had unprotected sex.

She could get pregnant.

With Cooper's baby.

The thought was mindboggling.

And thrilling.

And terrifying.

And thrilling.

"Shaye?"

She jolted out of her thoughts. "Sorry? What?"

Coop smiled. "You need to put your shirt on."

"Oh. Right." Reaching over she snagged the borrowed top. Slipping it over her head, she cursed her over-abundant breasts. Kelsey would be getting her shirt back stretched. Hopefully, it wasn't one of her friend's favorites. Although ruining Kelsey's clothes was the least of Shaye's problems right now.

COOP WATCHED SHAYE CLOSELY. She'd been quiet since they emerged from the bathroom. Even Kelsey's continuous questioning about the job she'd been offered couldn't get Shaye to speak in anything longer than a sentence at a time. And those were sparse of words.

He could tell she wanted to leave. She wasn't the only one. They needed to talk about what had happened. There was no way he was letting her move across the country without knowing if she was pregnant, and there was no way in hell she was going if she was.

They'd cross that bridge when they came to it, and if he wanted to rush out and buy a home pregnancy kit right now, who could blame him.

"You still haven't told us when you're actually going." Kelsey's words snapped Coop to attention.

Shaye shrugged. "I haven't nailed that down yet. But I need to be out of my house on the thirtieth of the month."

"But that's only four weeks away."

Coop sat up straight. He didn't like that anymore than Kelsey did.

"I know."

He really didn't like it. "So you leave in a month?"

She'd played him. Her time limit on them fitted with her moving away.

Oh, he *really* didn't like that. "When were you planning on telling us you were going? The day you leave?"

"No. I..." Shaye avoided his gaze and looked to Kelsey. "It's a dream job."

"I get that. But Shaye, it's not just a job you're accepting."

Kelsey leaned over and grabbed Shaye's hand, and Coop wanted to snatch it away and hold it himself. "You're uprooting your whole life."

"It's hardly a life right now. I'm unemployed. What do you expect me to do? Move in with you and West?"

"Yes."

"No!" Cooper shouted over Kelsey.

Shaye's gaze darted between him and Kelsey.

"What if you could get a full-time job? A live in one?" Coop asked. "You wouldn't have to worry about paying rent or utilities in exchange for work. Plus, you get a wage."

"What?"

The more the idea formed, the more perfect it seemed. "How are you at wielding a paintbrush? A sander?"

Kelsey and West looked at him with matching grins. Shaye on the other hand looked completely baffled.

"I know a job that pays well and comes with a room. There's even somewhere for you to store your stuff so you don't have to worry about storage costs." Oh yeah, he was really liking this idea.

"As a painter?" Shaye asked.

"It's just until you find what you're looking for here. In Sydney. You don't really want to go, or you would have taken that dream job already. And you haven't, have you?"

She shook her head. Bit her lip.

"So you take this job, have a roof over your head, money in your pocket and time whenever you need it to go to job interviews for what you're really after. There's no set hours with the job I'm offering."

"You're offering?" Shaye's brow wrinkled. "Cooper you're going to have to be more specific. I haven't a clue what it is you're talking about other than there's paint and a room involved somehow."

"I could use some help with doing up the house I bought last month. Normally, I pay some of my guys to do it on weekends and when I don't need them on other sites. Instead, you can do it. And I'll pay you labourer's wages." Damn. Coop couldn't believe how genius this idea was.

"So I'd live in this house? Is that possible?"

"Of course. Other than a day or two when I rip the kitchen out, it'll be completely livable the whole time."

"And I can store my things?"

God, was she going to say yes? Please let her say yes. "Yep. The garage is big enough to hold all your stuff, but you can also use whatever you want in the house. I haven't got much."

"You don't have much?" Little creases formed between Shaye's eyebrows.

"A couch, TV, bed." He shrugged. "I don't need much."

"Shaye, this is the perfect solution. You can still find a job in finance, but you can take your time doing it. Wait for the right one," Kelsey said.

"And you won't have to give up everything. I know how much time you and Kelsey spend together. There's no way either of you would cope if you lived on the other side of the country," West added.

Coop loved that Kelsey and West were backing him on this.

"And if I don't find a job before the house is finished?" Shaye asked.

"It'll take months to finish, and I'll have the next one lined up by then."

"Just so we're clear. I'll be your labourer and live in the house?"

He nodded. "Yep."

"I'll be working with you."

Coop continued to nod, a smile curling his mouth.

Shaye frowned. "And living with you."

7

SHAYE COULDN'T BELIEVE she'd said yes to Coop. She was supposed to be keeping her distance. Not getting closer.

It was Kelsey's fault. She'd badgered and badgered Shaye until the idea had seemed like a good one. Thank God, she was smart enough to put some boundaries on it.

She'd accepted on two conditions.

One, she wouldn't move in until her current lease ran out.

And two, she could still decide to take the job in Perth.

As much as she didn't want to move away from all her friends—and really, they were more family than friends—she couldn't decline the job yet. She might not be thrilled with the location, but she hadn't lied when she'd said it was a dream job.

She'd worked her arse off for a position like this. She should have had it at her last job, but they'd brought in a new CEO and things hadn't worked out as expected. Shaye hadn't told anyone the full details about the incidents that had resulted in her resigning from Mortimers.

Not even Kelsey.

Of course, the non-disclosure clause in her payout package

had something to do with that. Plus, Shaye wasn't sure she'd made the right decision in accepting the company's offer. But after months of dealing with inappropriate innuendoes and the final altercation that had resulted in her boss having a broken nose and bruised balls, Shaye had just wanted out. Fast.

The whole thing had left a bad taste in her mouth, and she couldn't face going to that office every day no matter what the company did to fix the situation. So she'd agreed to keep her mouth shut and take triple what her severance pay should have been for doing so. It made her feel dirty in a way. And a coward. She should have pressed charges. She should have...

Too late for second-guessing now though. It was water under the bridge.

"You're awfully quiet," Coop murmured.

She glanced over, found him looking straight ahead, his eyes on the road as he drove, but she knew he was aware of her —of her mood. "Thinking."

"About?"

"Whether I really want to risk ruining my manicure by sanding your walls."

He smiled. "I'll pay for weekly manicures."

Shaye laughed. "Have you seen my nails? The least of their worries is sandpaper."

"I've notice you chewing on them from time to time. Not that it stopped you from leaving scratch marks down my back."

Shaye gasped. "I did not!"

It was Coop's turn to laugh. "Okay, you might not have drawn blood, but it certainly stung when you came screaming in my ear."

"I did not scream." She huffed.

"We'll have to work on that."

Shaye swallowed as her throat constricted. How did so few words set her on fire?

Coop brought his truck to a stop. "We're here."

She looked out the window at the house they'd stopped in front of. It was an average single-story dwelling. Not unlike the rest of the houses on the street. But it looked sad. A little neglected. "This is it?"

"Yeah. Want the full tour?"

She'd asked him to drive by so she could see what he was offering. "If we go in there, are we going to keep our hands off each other?" Shaye wasn't about to place all the blame on Coop for their lack of restraint. They were as bad as each other.

"Maybe I should wait outside." He switched off the truck and got out. "C'mon. You can walk through while I grab some things from the garage."

Shaye unbuckled her seatbelt and opened her door. "Out of sight, out of mind."

Coop grabbed her wrist, spun her around and pressed her between his body and the side of the truck. "Make no mistake, Shaye, you are *never* out of mind."

He lowered his head and his mouth brushed hers. He swept back and forth. Light and sweet, it was such a contrast to their usual passionate kisses that Shaye's knees wobbled and her tummy dipped. Coop took his time, left his tongue out of it and totally seduced her with his gentle caresses.

By the time he lifted his head, she was breathing hard and wondering why in hell she'd wanted them to keep their hands off each other.

"That's to tide you over until later."

He let her go and walked away. Left her leaning against his truck because her weak knees didn't seem to want to hold her up and made his way to the front door. Before she got her breath back or her brain cells under the competent supervision of her common sense, Coop had opened the door and had gone inside.

Praying her legs wouldn't buckle, Shaye pushed away from the truck and walked up the path. Like the house, the yard could do with some care. The grass was long—knee height— and the weeds outnumbered the plants five to one.

The closer she got to the house, the more obvious the neglect. Paint peeled from around the windows and door. The cladding had seen better days, in sections it appeared split, and the little porch roof listed on one end. On closer inspection, she saw the support post had been propped up with some cut-off bits of timber.

"I'll fix that first." Cooper stepped through the front door. "No point inviting a lawsuit."

"It's that unsafe?"

"Nah, it's fine. Looks crap though." He grinned. "I'll be in the garage. Come get me when you're done."

Shaye watched him cross the yard to the garage and open the roller door, which rose with a screech of metal. She covered her ears with her hands but it wasn't quick enough to save her eardrums.

"That's on the list for next week too," Coop called out as he went inside.

She frowned. He'd said the place was livable, but Shaye was having doubts. Although she had to admit Coop was one of the few people she would trust with her life, so if he said it was safe, then it was. She'd still rather check it out herself. Not that she was qualified or anything. Unlike Cooper.

Sighing, she turned and stared through the front door. No point putting it off.

COOP TOOK HIS TIME. He wanted Shaye to take a good look at the house. It made no sense, but he wanted her to see what he did. The exterior might be a little shabby and need care, but underneath this place had the solid bones of a family home. Like the last place he'd flipped, he planned on sprucing it up and putting it on the market well over the price he'd paid.

He glanced at the house as he locked up the back of his truck. She'd been in there for ages. It didn't take that long to walk through the four-bedrooms and living space. Making his way to the front door, Coop tried to remember if he'd washed the dishes and picked up his dirty clothes.

Striding through the front door, he almost collided with Shaye. She was in the foyer, peeling the sailboat-covered wallpaper with her hands.

"You know, I have a special tool to help with that." He crossed his arms and watched her as she stripped a long section from the wall.

"Mmm..." She gripped another ragged edge and pulled.

"The wallpaper. I've got something to make removing it easier."

"Oh. I like doing it this way. It's...relaxing. Helps me think."

Relaxing? Peeling wallpaper? Was she mad? It was the one job Coop hated. Which was why he never put the stuff up. "Well, you're not working for me yet, so don't expect to get paid."

She paused. "I won't charge you for this." She ripped off another section with a hard yank.

Something was up. "Shaye?"

"This won't work." Another piece. Another yank.

"What? Peeling wallpaper off by hand?"

"No. Me. You."

Okay. "You'll have to be a little more specific."

"The first thing I thought about when I looked into your bedroom was messing up your bed."

"Ah—"

"And the shower in the master bathroom is big enough for two."

"Big enou—"

"Then there's the island in the kitchen. That thing is perfect for…" She finally looked at him. "See what I mean? This isn't going to work."

Coop wasn't sure what to say. Or think. All right, he knew what to think, he just wasn't supposed to be thinking it. But the wall she'd been stripping was solid. Strong. Definitely able to take the weight of both of them leaning against it while he fucked her.

He took a step towards her. She took one away. He took another one. "Shaye."

"Don't look at me like that."

"Like what?" He arched one eyebrow.

"Like you want to eat me whole."

Coop grinned. "Oh, no worries about that. I have no desire to eat you whole. I plan to eat you one nibble at a time."

"Coop—"

He pressed into her, making her move backwards, step after step until her back came up against the wall. She was breathing hard. So was he. Her face was flushed and those baby blues had disappeared—squeezed out by her dilated pupils.

His nostrils flared as he took a deep breath of her. She still smelled like sex. Neither of them had been able to shower after they'd fucked at West's house, and he loved that. Loved knowing the scent of them remained. Coop figured Shaye would wash him off the second she could, but for now he was all over her.

And he planned to drench her this time.

Soak so deep inside her that she'd never get him out.

"Cooper." She licked her lips—sent his pulse skyrocketing. "We can't."

"Can." He leaned against her, lowered his head until his jaw skimmed the side of her face. "You know you want to."

"But." She sucked in a breath when he swept his hand down her side and gripped her hip. "The rules. No hooking up at each other's places."

"I already told you I intend to break your rules," he murmured, brushing her ear with his lips.

She shuddered. "But—"

He was done arguing.

Turning his head, he swooped in and took her mouth. He put both hands on her hips and pulled her to her toes so their mouths fit together better. There was no protest. Only demand. She might say one thing, but her body said another.

Shaye wanted this as badly as he did. He thought he held the upper hand until she surrendered. Melting into him, she thrust her tongue between his lips and plundered. Except she didn't take. She offered. And right there, she had him on his knees.

If he couldn't convince her they were worth more than a month. Couldn't convince her to stay. Fuck. He couldn't think about it. Not now. He needed to use everything he had to make sure she wanted to stay in Sydney. Stay with him.

Coop thought about heading for his bedroom. For a second. Then she gripped him through his pants and all bets were off. He'd have her here. Against the wall. Hard and hot. Fast. Neither of them would be able to walk when he was done. But first, he wanted another taste of that sweet cunt.

He let go of her mouth and dropped to his knees. Shoved her skirt up and pulled her underwear out of the way. Her cunt glistened with her juices and he took a deep breath as he leaned in and swiped his tongue over her. She bucked. Hips rocking into him and hands in his hair, she took what she wanted. What she needed.

She curled her fingers in his hair tighter and he knew she was close. A few more strokes of his tongue, a thrust of his finger... Except he didn't want it to be his finger buried inside her when she came. He wanted her to come all over his cock.

Surging to his feet, Coop yanked at the button and zip on his pants. "Turn around."

Shaye did as she was told. She pressed her palms flat on the wall and tilted her hips to offer him that sweet arse. He wanted to fuck that. And he would. But not now. He was far too close to the edge to take it easy on her, and there was no way he'd risk hurting her.

Cock in hand, he moved in behind her, kicked her feet wider and bent his knees to line himself up. He pulled her thong out of the way and, with one thrust, he plunged deep. And she took him. All the way.

He felt the walls of her cunt sucking at him as he pulled out. Pushed in.

He'd been right. It was hard. It was hot. And it was fast.

So fast his head spun.

His knees shook and he powered his hips faster. Desperate to take them both over before his legs gave out. Reaching around Shaye, he slid his hand down her belly and his fingers over her clit. She pushed back against him, grinding her arse into his groin and shoving him straight into the fire.

He exploded with a growl and rammed his cock deep. Pulse after pulse surged through his length. Fire burst through him. His lungs seized and the hot wash of release rolled over him.

SHAYE ROSE to her toes when Cooper shoved deep and growled in her ear. The hard thrust along with the fingers stroking her clit set her orgasm off. She came. Wave after wave of throbbing pleasure that blurred her vision and shattered her sanity.

Breathing hard, she collapsed forward, the wall and Coop's body pressed against her, stopping her from crumpling to the floor. Her legs shook, her muscles feeling like warm jelly.

"Need to sit." Cooper's arms wrapped around her waist and guided her to the floor with him. Somehow, he managed to keep them connected. "We've got a problem."

Other than being brain-dead? "Huh?"

"I forgot again."

Forgot? Again? "Oh shit."

"I'm sorry." He pressed his lips to her shoulder and tightened his hold. "I've got no excuse. You should kick my arse."

She'd like to let Coop take all the blame. Pretend she had no say in any of this. Except that was a cop-out, and she knew it. "You're not the only responsible adult here."

"You can't leave."

"What?"

"Perth. The job. You can't take it."

Shaye's spine stiffened.

"Not when we don't know if you're pregnant." He cradled her in his lap, their bodies still joined. "You have to stay."

"I don't have to do any such thing." She gathered all her strength and climbed off Cooper. "You don't get to tell me what to do."

Scrambling to her feet, she tugged her skirt down. She might surrender to Coop's demands when it came to sex, but she wasn't about to let anyone, least of all Cooper Moreland, tell her what she could and couldn't do.

"C'mon, Shaye, be reasonable."

"R-re-reasonable?" She saw red. "Reasonable? I'll give you reasonable, you chauvinistic Neanderthal."

He held up his hands as he got to his feet. "Now wait a second."

"I'm not waiting for anything. It's my life and no one is going to force me to do something I don't want to." She pushed past him, headed for the door, but she only got a few steps before Coop grabbed her wrist and spun her back.

"I'm not forcing you to do anything." He let her go. "I would never do that, and you know it. So what's the real problem?"

She sucked in a breath. "I don't know what you're talking about."

One side of his mouth kicked up in a half smile. "You know, I think you might actually be telling the truth for once."

"What does that mean?" She didn't understand, and Cooper's knowing look only heightened her frustration and in turn, her anger. "If you've got something to say, then say it."

"It's not me saying you can't take that job that has you upset. It's that you don't really want to take it."

Her mouth dropped open. Snapped shut. Opened.

"You can put your rules on this—" he waved his hand between them, "—to hold me at arm's length. And you can pretend that the job is everything you're looking for, but it's a lie and we both know it."

"It is not!" Shaye crossed her arms over her chest. "It's a dream job."

"I bet it is. But it isn't *your* dream job, Shaye."

"Of course it is."

"No. Your dream job wouldn't have you uprooting the rest of your life, leaving behind the people that matter most to you, or have you unable to accept it the second it was offered."

"That's ridiculous."

"Is it?" He tilted his head and studied her carefully. "You know, I thought you were braver than this. The Shaye I know wouldn't let anyone shake her, never mind a spineless man who needs to use his superior position to cop a feel."

All the air left her lungs. How did Coop know about that? She'd told him and their friends about the inappropriate comments, but she'd never mentioned the contact—the touching.

Coop stepped closer. Ran a finger along her jaw. "The Shaye I know wouldn't be feeling cornered or desperate enough to accept a job that takes her away from everything and everyone she loves. My Shaye would do whatever necessary to live the life she wants."

"It's not that easy." God, she wished it was.

He smiled. "It is Shaye. You just have to make it happen."

"What if I can't?" There was so much at stake. In leaving. In staying.

"You can do it." He cupped her cheek. "I dare you to."

8

COOP HADN'T SEEN Shaye all week. He'd dropped her at her house Saturday night and heard not a peep since. And she'd not been home the five times he'd gone by.

He was so antsy his skin itched.

He'd called West. Pumped his friend for info, and when that had gotten him nothing, he'd called Kelsey. She'd given up less than West. Seemed his prediction of girlfriends sticking together had come to fruition.

The wallpaper in the foyer mocked him whenever he left or entered the house, and he'd been so agitated that he'd been unable to get anything done. At work or home. All he thought about was Shaye and how he missed her. How much he wanted her here helping him turn this house into a home a family would love.

And that only made him think about fucking her without protection and that she could be walking around right now carrying his kid and he wouldn't know.

Because she wouldn't talk to him.

It was Friday, and as soon as he locked up, he was hunting

down Shaye and dragging her back here so they could have this out once and for all. She wasn't leaving. He'd tie her to his bed if he had to.

Of course, he'd be sure to drive her mad with pleasure while she was there. He'd make it impossible for her to walk away from what they had.

Lord knows, he couldn't.

He'd probably been in denial for years because he'd always felt a pull towards Shaye. He'd just been a dumbarse and not recognised what that tug meant.

He was in love with her.

So deep in love that he couldn't live without her, and if that meant he had to use every trick he had to keep her here, he would. And if he failed to make her want to stay, he'd follow.

The thought of uprooting his life, leaving behind a prosperous business—his family—didn't deliver the pain that giving up Shaye did.

That right there told him all he needed to know.

He might have been slow on the uptake, but now that he'd seen the light, he'd move heaven and earth to get what he wanted.

Shaye.

Forever.

Except the best plans always got waylaid.

Opening the door, he came face-to-face with West. "Hey. What are you doing here?"

"Got kicked out of home."

"What?" West had to be joking. "Kelsey kicked you out?"

West laughed. "Don't look so stricken. It's only for the night. She's having a girls' night, and seeing how I'm equipped with a cock, I'm not invited."

"Oh, right."

"Are you going to invite me in?"

"Ah, well, I was on my way out."

"Yep. I bet you were." West shoved past and entered the house. "But you won't be getting close to what you were going out for right now."

Coop arched an eyebrow at his friend and closed the door. "You got a crystal ball now?"

"No. But Shaye's at my house with Kelsey, and there's no breaching those walls by individuals with cocks tonight."

"That bad?"

"I think they're plotting. Or implementing." West shrugged. "There's been a lot of whispered conversations this week, and I'm not really sure what's going on. Hell, they could be planning to take over the world and have a tank parked in my garage and if Kelsey doesn't want me to know, you can bet your arse I won't."

"Not knowing would drive me insane." Coop led the way to the kitchen.

"I don't need to know everything. I know the important stuff. Kelsey loves me, and if she were planning world domination, she'd be taking me with her. No doubt on that."

"I'm not lucky enough to have that kind of knowledge." Coop opened the fridge and held up a beer. "You want one?"

West nodded. "What knowledge?"

"That the woman I love loves me." Cooper handed over a beer and cracked one for himself. "I don't know a damn thing."

"You don't know?" West gave him an are-you-stupid look. "Well, shit. No wonder they're plotting."

"What does that mean?" What did his best friend know that he didn't? Because it was obvious that West knew something.

"You're telling me you have no idea how Shaye feels about you?"

"She's hot for me. We can't be in a room together without being all over each other."

"We all know that. You two have been sparking for months, but that's not what I'm talking about."

"What then?"

"She's in love with you."

"Huh?" *Shaye is in love with me?* "Since when?"

"Years."

"What?" Coop's voice had gone up an octave or two.

"Well, maybe not *in love*, but she's had a thing for you for as long as I can remember. You've been too blind to see it. Or stupid."

Shaye has a thing for me?

Stupid.

He'd been stupid. So fucking dense he'd wasted years where he could have had Shaye all to himself. "Fuck." Coop spun around, headed for the door.

"Not so fast, buddy." West grabbed the collar of Coop's shirt and pulled him to a stop. "Sit down and think about it. Shaye's got a heap of shit to sort through right now. You can't just go barrelling in there."

He swung back to face West. "The hell I can't. Don't you get it? Nothing else matters but me and her. The rest is incidental. It'll work itself out once we're straight. And we're going be straight because I'm not spending one more night without her in my bed."

West looked at his beer. "Right. So I'm not finishing this then."

"Up to you, but I'm out of here."

"No beer and storming the castle." West shook his head and sighed. "I swear, if you fuck this up and I end up going without sex again, you're a dead man."

Cooper laughed thinking about when Kelsey had held out

on West during Coop's brother's rough road to happy-ever-after with West's sister Freddie.

His friend needn't worry. Coop had no intention of coming home alone.

And the only thing he planned to fuck was Shaye.

SHAYE SPRANG to her feet as Cooper charged into Kelsey's living room.

"What the fuck, Coop? West!" Kelsey yelled.

West entered the room at a lazy stroll. His hands were up in front of him. "Don't yell at me. I'm just here so he doesn't break the front door down."

Shaye looked back at Coop. His fists were clenched at his sides. A muscle in his jaw ticked, his nostrils flared and his eyes...shit. Whatever the hell was going on, West was right. There was no stopping Coop.

"Get in the truck. We're going home." He spoke through clenched teeth.

"Cooper."

"Now, Shaye."

She could see the restraint. See the control he had over himself and knew he was close to breaking. Shaye didn't want to break him.

"I'll grab my bag."

"Shaye." Kelsey grabbed her hand. "You don't have to go."

She smiled at her friend and then glanced at Coop. "Yeah. I do."

"But—"

Shaye pulled Kelsey into a hug. "I'll call you, but you know I'll be fine with Cooper. He'd never do anything to hurt me."

Kelsey squeezed her tight. "I know that. Just don't let him bully you into anything you don't want."

She laughed. "I think he might want what I do, Kels."

"If he doesn't, he's an idiot." Kelsey let her go and turned to Coop. "Do. Not. Fuck. Her. Over."

Coop nodded but didn't speak. His eyes remained glued to Shaye.

Taking his unspoken message, she left the room to get her bag. It didn't take her long to pull her stuff together. She'd only brought the bare essentials to Kelsey's last weekend. Everything else was still at her house. Waiting for her to make a decision on her future.

It looked like that decision was getting made tonight.

She entered the hallway to find Coop waiting by the front door.

"Let's go." He held out his hand.

Shaye took it without hesitation and let him lead her out to the truck.

They were quiet on the drive. Both of them lost in their own thoughts. Shaye's centred on how she was going to tell him that she'd fallen in love with him. That she'd probably been in love with him when she'd suggested their thirty-day affair.

She was still wondering how to start the conversation when Coop pulled up in front of his house.

"Inside."

To an outsider, Coop would sound angry. But Shaye knew him well enough to know he was holding himself tight. Waiting until he was able to unleash whatever it was swirling inside him. And it wasn't anger.

She'd seen the hungry look in his eyes at Kelsey's. There might be a little irritation in there, and Shaye figured that stemmed from frustration more than anything. She was feeling a small amount of frustration herself. Of course, hers was aimed at herself, not him.

Unfortunately, Shaye had the feeling Coop's annoyance was aimed at her too.

She sighed. Grabbing her bag, she exited the truck and followed Coop into the house.

"Go put your bag in my room."

His order had her stumbling. "What?"

"My room. *Our* room."

"Cooper."

He held up a hand. "No. Don't say a word. I don't what to hear any arguments before you put that bag away."

"But I—"

"Shaye."

He didn't yell. He didn't have to. It was all in the tone, the way he looked at her. Coop could make her do anything with that voice.

She headed for the bedroom where she deposited her bag just inside the door. Making her way back to the foyer, she wondered what it meant that he wanted her bag in his room. She knew what she hoped it meant.

"I'm in the kitchen," Coop called.

When Shaye entered the kitchen, she came to a complete stop. Cooper was pulling food from the fridge. "What are you doing?"

"Getting stuff out for dinner. I've got steak. Thought I'd chargrill some veggies to go with it."

Okay. This was surreal. "Um..."

He glanced over. "You're not hungry?"

"No. Yes." She shook her head. "What are we doing?"

Coop straightened, unloaded his armful of food on the counter and walked towards her. When he stood right in front of her, he just stared. For ages.

"What?"

"I have no idea where to start."

"About?" She licked her lips. Swallowed through the lump suddenly lodged in her throat. Shaye was sure it was her heart. In fact, the thing must have broken apart and travelled to various parts of her body to pound like a team of miniature jackhammers.

"Us."

"Oh."

"You can't go to Perth, because I can't let you."

"I don't—"

He placed two fingers over her mouth. "Let me have my say, then you can have yours."

Shaye nodded.

"I've been an idiot. I never knew, and believe me, out of everything that's happened between us, that's the one thing I'm sorry for."

She had no idea what he was talking about.

"If I'd known what you were feeling, what the tug I felt whenever I was around you meant, I'd have done something about it, Shaye."

Air rushed through her teeth as she sucked in a breath. "Who told you?"

"West." Coop smiled. "He took great pleasure in calling me stupid."

She'd just bet he did. "I didn't know he knew. I tried to hide it."

"Why?"

Shaye shrugged. "When we first met, you were dating someone, so there was no way I was making a move."

"I've been single a lot of times over the years."

"Yeah, and you've been taken just as many too." She smiled. "I can't explain it really. It became a habit to hide how I felt. To live with just the fantasies I conjured up."

Cooper groaned. "Do not tell me you fantasised about us

being together. No. Wait. Do tell me, but not yet. Once we get things sorted out, I plan to make every one of your fantasies come true."

Shaye's insides clenched. "We should get back on topic."

"We're still on topic." He stepped closer, cupped her face in his work-roughened hands. "What's your heart's greatest desire? What does Shaye Adams want for now? For the future?"

"I want a job. In my field of expertise."

"Besides that. Where do you see yourself in five years? Ten?"

Could she tell him? He seemed to want more than the thirty days she's set, but... "I..."

"C'mon, Shaye. Tell me."

"You. I want to be with you." She bit her lip.

Cooper grinned. "What else do you want?"

She'd gone this far, there was no point stopping now. Taking a deep breath, she blurted, "Everything."

He outright smiled now. "I can help you get it all, but you have to take a chance. I want everything in return." Coop brushed his lips over hers. "Give it to me, Shaye. I dare you to."

EPILOGUE

"FOR FUCKS SAKE, Shaye, just pee on the stick!" Coop yelled through the bathroom door.

"I don't think I can," she yelled back.

"You gotta go, right?" How hard could it be? Pee, dip the stick and wait.

"It seems pointless..."

He knew what she meant. She was three weeks late. All signs pointed to her being pregnant. But they needed to *know.* "Shaye."

"I know. I know. Just pee on the stick."

She went quiet for long minutes. He almost gave in and put his ear to the door, but he held back. This wasn't a deal-breaker for them, but it would change everything.

They'd spent the last four weeks moving Shaye into the house and meshing their lives. She'd had a job interview that looked promising just this past week, but until she got an offer she was happy with, she worked for him.

Coop loved working with her on renovating the house. She had a good eye and she was a hard worker, listened when she didn't know how to do something and needed him to show her. The place was coming together. And with each new splash of paint, new appliance and blind, the house became theirs.

He didn't think they'd be flipping this one. It felt like home.

The door opened in front of him. Shaye stood there, an arm wrapped around her waist, the other bent at the elbow with her hand to her mouth so she could chew a nail.

"Hey." Coop moved to her, rescued her nail from certain death. "None of that. Whatever happens. We're good."

"I know." She sighed and wrapped her arms around his waist, laid her head on his chest. "I don't want to look."

"Why?"

"Because right now it's this vague possible *thing*, but once we look at that stick... God."

"We'll cope with whatever happens. Together."

"I know." Shaye sighed again. "I seem to be saying that a lot."

"I love you, Shaye. Whether you're carrying my kid or not won't change that."

"I still can't look." She squeezed his waist.

He chuckled. "C'mon. Take a look. I dare you to."

SHAYE TOOK a deep breath and slipped out of Cooper's arms. She grabbed his hand and wove her fingers through his. "Together?"

"Together."

They stepped into the bathroom and moved to the counter where she'd left the stick. "Is it time?"

"Oh yeah, it's time."

She glanced up to see him grinning. Except he wasn't looking at her. His gaze was trained on the countertop. Oh

God. Turning her head, Shaye squeezed her eyes shut and tried to build up the courage to look at that stupid pee-coated stick.

Positive.

Oh my God.

She was pregnant.

Her knees wobbled and her head spun. Black flecks flashed in her vision. "I think I'm going to faint."

Coop scooped her up in his arms and carried her back into the bedroom. He turned and fell backwards onto the bed. They didn't talk. Just lay in each other's arms for long minutes.

"Well, I guess we need to rethink the theme for one of the bedrooms," Cooper murmured.

"We're staying here?"

His shoulder lifted beneath her head. "If you want to."

"I like it here." And she did.

She'd met a couple of the neighbouring families and she had to admit she'd gotten attached to them quickly. Especially the kids. They were always playing in the street in the afternoons. She wanted that.

"What are you thinking about?"

"Staying here. Raising a family here." Her tummy dipped. Fluttered.

Cooper hugged her close. "I like that."

"What?"

"Raising a family. With you."

Shaye tipped her head back to look at him. "Kinda got no choice now." She frowned.

"None of that." He rubbed the crease between her eyebrows. "I want this with *you*. No one else."

"I still can't believe we did this. We got pregnant in Kelsey and West's bathroom."

"Nope." He shook his head. "I prefer to think it happened here. In the foyer. Against the wall."

She smiled. It could have happened either of those two times. They'd been so careful after that. Of course, it had been too late. The deed had been done. "We're having a baby." Saying the words out loud might help it sink in.

"That's what the stick says."

"I'm not sure I can believe it."

Coop laughed. "Well you better get sure. There's going to be a small bump making itself known in the very near future."

"Eight months."

"It'll be making itself known long before that." He rolled her to her back, placed his hand over her flat belly. "I can't wait to feel you grow."

"Grow fatter?"

"You're not fat. You've got curves in all the right places. And I love every inch of them."

She knew he did. The proof was in the fact he couldn't keep his hands off her. Especially her boobs. Cooper was definitely a boob man. Of course, they were bigger and bound to continue to grow with her pregnancy.

It was hard to believe the man she'd held a secret crush on for so long had fallen for her. She had gotten everything she'd always wished for.

All because she'd dared to.

ABOUT THE AUTHOR

Rhian Cahill is the alter ego of a former stay-at-home mother of four. With motherly duties rapidly dwindling Rhian is able to make use of the fertile imagination she used to keep herself sane for all those years of slavery. Having spent years living overseas and visiting tropical climates has helped inspire some steamy stories.

Multi-published in erotic romance and contemporary romance, Rhian, with the help of Mr. Muse, spends her days and nights writing.

When not glued to the keyboard you'll find her book or knitting in hand avoiding any and all housework as much as possible.

For more on Rhian –

Website – http://www.rhiancahill.com/
Newsletter signup – http://eepurl.com/byrsf
Twitter – https://twitter.com/RhianCahill
FaceBook – https://www.facebook.com/RhianCahillAuthor
Instagram – http://instagram.com/rhiancahill/
BookBub – https://www.bookbub.com/authors/rhian-cahill
Goodreads page - https://www.goodreads.com/rhian_cahill

MAD LOVE

HEARTS ARE WILD

History teacher Madison Keibler is aloof, uptight, prim and proper—and Toby Moreland's unlikely obsession. He doesn't understand why the newest staff member at their private high school intrigues him, he only knows he has a burning need to loosen her severe bun, strip her of those dowdy schoolmarm clothes and dirty her up a bit. As the shy, naïve Mad becomes his own personal bad girl, she quickly goes from the woman he can't stop touching, to the woman he can't live without.

A sheltered only child raised by cold, scholarly parents, Madison's been a student most of her life. Now Toby's giving her the education she never knew she was missing. And not just sex, though his expertise in that area could fill volumes. He's given her dozens of new experiences, from the joys of a simple walk on the beach at sunset, to the excitement of live sports, to what it's like to be part of a big, boisterous, loving family. For the first time in her life, she's living in the moment and loving every second.

But the ultimate experience for both may be sacrifice, after a single careless second threatens to destroy their new, crazy, unexpected *mad love*.

http://www.rhiancahill.com/books/hearts-are-wild/mad-love/

LOOK FOR THESE TITLES BY RHIAN CAHILL

Hearts Are Wild Series

No More Talking (novella)

Dare You To (novella)

Mad Love

Coyote Hunger Series

Coyote Home – Book 1

Coyote Wild – Book 2

Coyote Whispers – Book 3

Coyote Law – Book 3.5

Coyote Lies – Book 4

Party Games Series

Truth Or Dare

Spin The Bottle

Pass The Parcel – Novella

Are You Game Series

7 Minutes In Heaven – Book 1

Catch'n'Kiss – Book 2

Red Light, Green Light – Book 3

For a full list of Rhian's available books visit her website

http://www.rhiancahill.com/books/

www.ingramcontent.com/pod-product-compliance
Lightning Source LLC
Chambersburg PA
CBHW031022190726
48286CB00003BA/975